D1452303

Tamworth Pig Stories

by the same author

Stories about Cricklepit Combined School

THE TURBULENT TERM OF TYKE TILER
(Awarded the Library Association's Carnegie Medal)

GOWIE CORBY PLAYS CHICKEN

CHARLIE LEWIS PLAYS FOR TIME

JUNIPER

JASON BODGER AND THE PRIORY GHOST

NO PLACE LIKE

I CAN'T STAND LOSING

DOG DAYS AND CAT NAPS

MR MAGUS IS WAITING FOR YOU

THE CLOCK TOWER GHOST

THE WELL

TAMWORTH PIG AND THE LITTER

CHRISTMAS WITH TAMWORTH PIG

Edited by Gene Kemp

DUCKS AND DRAGONS
Poems for Children

ff

TAMWORTH
PIG
STORIES

Gene Kemp

Illustrated by Carolyn Dinan

faber and faber
LONDON · BOSTON

First published in 1987
by Faber and Faber Limited
3 Queen Square London WC1N 3AU

Printed in Great Britain by
Richard Clay Ltd, Bungay, Suffolk

Text first published by Faber and Faber
Limited
as *The Prime of Tamworth Pig* (1972) and
Tamworth Pig Saves the Trees (1973)

*British Library Cataloguing in Publication
Data*

Kemp, Gene
Tamworth Pig stories.
I. Title   II. Dinan, Carolyn
III. Kemp, Gene. The prime of
Tamworth Pig
IV. Kemp, Gene. Tamworth Pig saves
trees
823'.914[J]   PZ7

ISBN 0-571-14931-6

For Eva
With love and thanks

Contents

---------------✷---------------

Ah! Tamworth Pig is a very fine pig
  The best you'll ever see,
His ears stand up, his snout is long,
  His score is twenty-three.
He's wise and good and big and bold,
  And clever as can be,
A faithful friend to young and old
  The Pig of Pigs is he.

By courtesy of Mr. Rab

". . . Pigs of the Tamworth breed . . . are creatures of enchantment. . . ."

Anonymous pig-fancier

The Prime of Tamworth Pig

Chapter One

Thomas sat on top of a grassy hill on a warm, windy, April afternoon.

"Yoicks," he shouted into the breeze.

He felt wonderful, having just recovered from mumps, measles, chicken-pox, German measles, scarlatina and whooping cough. But, at last, he was better; there didn't appear to be much left to catch and the doctor had said he needn't go back to school till September.

"Just let him run wild," were his words.

"If he's at home running wild, then I shall go to school to keep out of his way," Daddy had replied.

Thomas bellowed to the fields and hedges all around:

> "*No more school, mouldy old school,*
> *No more school and sorrow,*
> *Lots and lots of holidays*
> *Before there comes tomorrow.*"

He rolled over and over down the hill at the sheer bliss of his thought, followed closely by Hedgecock and Mr. Rab who were arguing as usual.

"You're not in the least like a real rabbit. Don't make me laugh."

"Yes, I am. I am. Say I am, please. Just a bit like one."

Hedgecock snorted loudly.

"I never saw a real rabbit with a red and white striped waistcoat, a green bow tie, and skinny, pink, furry legs. You're enough to make a cat laugh—to say nothing of a real rabbit."

"Well, what about you? What are you, then? A hedgecock with feathery prickles. You can't fly and you can't prickle."

"But I'll tell you what I can do. I can bash you, Stripey."

He proceeded to do so. Mr. Rab roared with pain. He was no match for Hedgecock.

"Stop that," Thomas commanded. "I'll do the bashing round here. Come on. What shall we do?"

"The stream," Hedgecock said. "We'll go to the stream."

"Yes, to the stream; let's go."

They ran over the grass, Mr. Rab trying to dodge the daisies; he was soft-hearted over flowers, over everything in fact, except Hedgecock, and he hated treading on daisies.

Suddenly they were there. Banks, two or three feet high, covered with mossy rocks just right for sitting on, bordered the clear water. The trio sniffed eagerly. It smelt good, as ever. Perhaps it was the bracken, or the wild thyme, or perhaps it was just the stream itself that gurgled over the brown stones on the sandy bed. The path ran into a curving bay and stepping-stones crossed to the other side. Farther down there was a stretch of grassy turf covered with molehills and mole-holes. Thomas walked into the water, still with his shoes and socks on, and tried to catch minnows shooting this way and that. Then he sat down on a stone and contemplated his feet (over which the stream rippled making very interesting patterns) for some time.

"I know, let's make a dam," he said at last.

They chose a spot where the stream narrowed between high banks. Hedgecock worked steadily, counting the large stones (four-five-six-seven-eight-nine-ten-eleven) as he carried them to Thomas, who rammed them into position against the log they'd pushed across the stream. Mr. Rab was ordered to plaster mud and sand into the gaps. He whimpered to himself, for the water was cold and his paws hurt. Water still rushed through the spaces between the stones but its colour was turning to a reddish-brown, and gradually it slowed down and began to spread out on the flat, grassy ground above the dam.

Mr. Rab sat on a rock, tucking his wet paws under his waistcoat, and stuck his thin legs into the sun-warmed grass. The other two ignored him, as they continued to stuff pebbles, mud and grass into every crack. Mr. Rab began to recite in his special voice that he kept for poetry, which was a kind of high, wobbly moan.

> "*There's a stream on a grassy common*
> *Runs very swift and clear. . . .*"

"You can cut that lot out," Hedgecock shouted. "I hate your rotten poetry. If you've enough energy to say that old rubbish, then you'd better come and help."

But Mr. Rab wasn't listening. "Look! Look!" he shrieked.

The others turned round to see why he was dancing about and pointing a quivering paw. Upstream of the dam, the water was now several feet wide and all the moleholes had disappeared beneath it. There on the grass, shaking their fists, were dozens of angry moles.

"You horrible beasts," the Chief Mole shouted, leaping from one damp foot to the other. "You've wrecked our homes. You nearly drowned us all."

"We didn't mean . . ." Thomas began.

"Yes you did. You did it on purpose. I know you. We all know you. Terrible Thomas, that's who you are; you—you—you——"

The mole spluttered with rage and wetness.

Mr. Rab was dashing the tears from his eyes and Hedgecock was trying to hide in the bracken.

"I'm sorry," Thomas muttered. "We'll undam: I mean, we'll knock it down. Hedgecock, stop creeping away. Come and help."

With one accord, they and the moles all began to demolish the dam. It came down much faster than it went up, Hedgecock noted bitterly. Soon the stream was flowing as noisily and happily as before.

"It will be all right now," the Chief Mole said. "We shall dry out in the sun. I don't think you meant it after all."

"No, we didn't."

"Next time, build farther up there and then it won't affect us."

"But will there be a next time?" Mr. Rab moaned. "Look at us."

Silently they inspected one another: wet, scratched, plastered with mud. Thomas had torn his trousers and lost his shoes and socks.

"Come on, there's going to be trouble," he said.

At that moment two figures leapt from the bank and pushed Thomas flat into the stream. Even as his head was held down into the cold water, while their feet kicked him, Thomas knew who they were—Christopher Robin Baggs (most unsuitably named), a spotty boy with stick-out teeth, and his rough, tough friend, Lurcher Dench, both enemies of Thomas. He had fought many battles with them, but he had thought they were at school today, and so he had not been on the look-out. He squirmed and struggled and kicked under their combined weight. Then one of them stood on his legs. It hurt.

"Let's drown old Twopenny Tom," they were yelling. "Down with Measle Bug."

Somehow he got his face out of the water. Hedge-cock was snapping and biting but Mr. Rab had disappeared. The rage inside Thomas was bubbling like a boiling cauldron. Fancy letting himself be caught like this and without shoes. He couldn't have been more defenceless. The terrible thought shot through his head that perhaps they really did intend to drown him, as Lurcher once more ground his face down into the sand and water. There was a roaring in Thomas's ears and stars shot across the blankness that was enveloping him. The roaring crescendoed into a mighty sound that was somehow not in his head and as if by magic, the weight lifted off him, the kicks and blows and the pain ceased, and he stood up shakily to see the backs of his attackers running away as if pursued by demons. Mr. Rab's soft paws were stroking his sore legs as Thomas stumbled forward to his rescuer.

There on the bank stood a huge, golden pig, a giant of a pig, the colour of beech leaves in autumn, with upstanding, furry ears and a long snout.

"Tamworth!" Thomas gasped, spitting out water, sand and the odd tooth. "Oh! Tamworth, I am pleased to see you. How did you know?"

"Mr. Rab fetched me—ran like the wind, he did. I

14

wasn't far away. Funny the way those two objection-
able boys fled when they saw me. I can't think why.
I'm a most amiable animal and I don't believe in
violence."

"I ache all over," Thomas said, investigating his
bruises.

"Up on my back, all of you. Home we must go.
Your mother will undoubtedly have a few words to
say. Humph! Don't wet all my bristles."

"Giddy-up, Tamworth," Thomas said, holding
tight to the golden back.

Thomas's mother did, in fact, have a great many
things to say when he arrived home; she went on and
on for a considerable time. Later, he lay very carefully

in bed because of his many bruises, and buried his face in Num. To everyone else, Num was just a piece of shabby, grey blanket but to Thomas, Num was warmth and softness and comfort in times of sorrow. Wriggling gingerly into the welcoming folds, he said to Mr. Rab:

"Sing a bedtime song."

"Not that old muck," Hedgecock growled.

"Go and count your squares if you don't want to hear it."

Hedgecock retired muttering to the blanket of knitted squares at the foot of the bed. There were eight one way and ten the other, all in different

colours. Hedgecock loved to count them in tens, or twos, or ones.

Mr. Rab sang reedily. This was a special poem and he'd made up a tune to it, of which he was very proud.

> "*Mr. Rab has gone to sleep*
> *Tucked in his tiny bed*
> *He has curled up his furry paws*
> *And laid down his sleepy head.*"

"Seventy-eight, seventy-nine, eighty," droned Hedgecock. Then there was a loud snore as he, like the others, fell asleep.

Chapter Two

———————————*———————————

Blossom, Thomas's sister, had a day's holiday from
school and so got up very early, full of cheer. She laid
the breakfast, took tea to Mummy and Daddy and then
woke up Thomas to play a game of Monopoly.
Thomas liked games but hated to lose and he hated
paying out any money so from time to time he would
rush from the room roaring and stamping with rage.
Then, having simmered down, he would come back.

Blossom remained quite unperturbed by all this,
merely continuing with her book till his return. She
was a round, brown-eyed girl, rather like an otter, with
an amiable disposition and a kind heart. Like Mr. Rab
she loved poetry and hated sums. She couldn't understand, at all, Thomas's wish to win everything. In a
good game winning didn't matter. She was as warm
and comfortable as a bed at the end of a tiring day and
sometimes silly, with a great and glorious silliness, just
to show she wasn't too saintly after all.

The game came to an end with Thomas hurling the
board across the room as he was obviously going to
lose. Money, dice, tokens, houses, hotels flew through
the air.

"I hate that stupid game," he shouted.

"Only because you're losing," Blossom said calmly, picking up the debris.

They then went down to breakfast, and afterwards set off for Baggs's orchard to see Tamworth Pig, for he always welcomed visitors and conversation. Tamworth belonged to Farmer Baggs, whom he liked, but was looked after by Mrs. Baggs—a mean woman—whom he hated. Christopher Robin Baggs we have already encountered. His warfare with Tamworth and Thomas had gone on for a long time, dating probably from the time when he'd tried to set fire to Tamworth's straw to see how quickly the pig could move. Actually it was Christopher who did the moving, pursued by an inflammatory Tamworth.

When Blossom and Thomas arrived, Tamworth was deep in conversation with Joe the Shire-horse.

"The price of pig food has gone up again, Joe. It's ridiculous. Mrs. Baggs hardly gives me a decent meal as it is, just a lot of old scraps, scarcely sufficient to maintain a budgerigar in good health. Now I suppose she'll give me even less. Hello, Blossom. Hello, Thomas. Have you heard? The price of pig food is up, and eggs and butter are to cost more. And this isn't necessary. The economic situation of this country is due entirely to inefficiency. Now, if I were Prime Minister, everything would soon be different."

"Why? What would you do then?" Joe asked slowly.

New ideas were always difficult for Joe.

"Well, I'd put the most important thing first."

"And what's that?"

"Why, food, of course," Tamworth said. "We can't live without food. We can't work without food. Food keeps us going and I also think it's one of the best things in life. The very best possibly."

"I believe you're right," Blossom agreed.

She felt in her anorak pocket for a toffee that she seemed to remember leaving there, for she dearly loved to eat.

"I've brought some apples for you."

Thomas emptied the contents of his brown paper bag on the floor.

"They're a bit wormy, but all right."

Tamworth gobbled them down and then continued speaking.

"Well, then, since food is the most important thing in life we should gear our whole existence to its production. Think, for example, of all the waste ground in this country. It should all be used to grow more food, potatoes, mushrooms, peas, lettuce, tomatoes, onions and lovely cabbage. Children should be taught to grow and make as much food as possible. Everyone could make more sweets, toffees and chocolates, and cakes, and biscuits, and buns and bread, and there would be lots and lots for everyone. We could even send tons of food abroad to feed the starving people."

"What about the 'orses?" Joe asked. "What about my 'ay?"

Joe had a one-track mind which seldom moved far from the thought of hay.

"Tons of hay go to waste every year on the grass verges by the sides of the roads. It should all be used. Extra food, better food could then be given to all the cows and hens, who would give more butter, cheese and eggs. More of everything for everybody except MEAT. Meat," Tamworth repeated firmly, "is bad for everyone."

Tamworth's feelings about meat were very strong.

"Yes, that should be our country's motto. MAKE

MORE FOOD. And if I ever become Prime Minister, it will be the first point on my programme."

"GROW MORE GRUB would sound better," Thomas suggested.

A voice was heard calling for Joe and he lumbered away, brooding on the prospect of unlimited hay.

"Tamworth," Blossom said slowly, "you're known as a very wise pig. Tell me, how can we make some money?"

"Why do you ask?"

"Well, you know, I think we must be very poor because every time I want something, Mummy says, 'Do you think I'm made of money?' and Daddy's always grumbling about bills and income tax. And then Gwendolyn Twitchie has twice as much pocket money as I do."

"And you have twice as much as me," Thomas grumbled. "It's not fair."

"I'm older than you."

"Yes, but you're much more stupid, so I ought to get as much as you."

"Stop arguing," Tamworth commanded. "I shall have to give this some thought. Have you got another apple?"

"No, you've eaten them all."

"Well, it's time for my morning nap now. Call again soon and I'll let you know if I've thought of anything. Oh, and can you draw lots of posters with 'Make More Food' on them, and I'll get them distributed. I feel I must start a campaign, in view of this rise in the price of pig food."

He turned round twice in his comfortable quarters, pushed his straw into a heap and flopped down.

"Scratch my back, please, Thomas. The stick's over there."

Thomas scratched the bristly, golden back and Tamworth closed his eyes in contentment. Soon a gentle, whiffling noise filled the air.

"He's asleep," Blossom whispered.

Tamworth opened one small, bright eye.

"I'm not. I'm thinking, Good-bye."

They wandered slowly home. The sun was shining. It was a beautiful day.

"Let's play in the tree-house with Hedgecock and Mr. Rab," Thomas said.

"All right."

And they raced back to the house singing "Green grow the rushes–oh!"

After that the day suddenly went wrong for Thomas, for who should be awaiting Blossom but Gwendolyn Twitchie. Instantly Blossom turned into a different creature.

"Let's be princesses," they squawked and ran giggling into the bedroom.

Thomas banged on the door and shouted, "Let me in, you stupid fools!" but they only tittered and piled things against the door so that he couldn't shift it at all. He fetched his hammer in order to batter it down, but Daddy appeared, roaring like a lion. He sent Thomas into the garden, where he wandered dismally into the tree-house with Mr. Rab and Hedgecock. They couldn't seem to start off a good game, but sat arguing feebly, making patterns in the dust with their shoes.

Suddenly Daddy came up to them.

"You seem miserable, Thomas. Oh, yes, of course, Blossom's got that awful child with her. Here, go and buy yourself something with this."

Thomas ran to the nearest shop, where he purchased a particularly sticky bar of toffee which he ate all over the house, putting his fingers everywhere. He didn't realize he was doing this; he was just thinking of all the horrible names he would like to call Gwendolyn, but Mummy found the traces.

"Look at the mess you've made and the hall's just been painted. Now go upstairs and wash your hands, and clean your teeth while you're about it. They're like yellow fangs."

The toothpaste was minty and frothy. Thomas used a lot of it, building up a fine lather. He stuck his head

25

out of the window and surveyed the garden. Everything was growing beautifully and he could see the most marvellous red and yellow tulip.

"I wonder if I can spit in it?" he thought, leaning far out of the window and taking careful aim.

At that very moment, Daddy chose to walk along the path and the frothy cloud dropped on his head and started to trickle into his eyes. The roar this time was really awe-inspiring, like fifty lions. Thomas crouched down under the bathroom window. Too late he thought of seeking refuge elsewhere. Daddy, like an avenging Thor with his thunderbolt, loomed large and terrible in the doorway, wiping off large quantities of toothpaste.

"Bed," he remarked grimly, "is the only place for you today."

He scooped Thomas under one arm, carried him into his room and dumped him on the bed.

"Don't dare get up till I tell you."

He closed the door and stamped off.

Thomas lay in misery. All the beauty of the day had gone. Mr. Rab crept down beside him and tried to sing the bedtime song.

"Shut up, you idiot. It's morning."

Hedgecock was counting up to a thousand in tens, but Thomas didn't care. He buried his face in Num and tried to sleep.

He was allowed up for lunch and sat quietly while Gwendolyn and Blossom chattered gaily. Gwendolyn was the daughter of Blossom's teacher and was said to be very clever.

"I'm reading a very difficult book just now," she informed them all.

Blossom looked at her admiringly. Thomas pushed his plate away, for Gwendolyn put him off his food, and, besides, he was very full of toffee.

After lunch he put out his lines for Percy, the small engine, and watched him, but the busy, chuffing train could not hold his attention for long. He heard the girls laughing in the garden and he lay on his back and drummed with his heels. Mr. Rab tried to pat his head but he pushed the soft paw away. Then Mummy came in.

"I thought we'd have a picnic on the lawn as it's such a lovely day. Oh, do stop kicking, Thomas, and cheer up."

Thomas sat up.

"Can we have ice-cream and sausages on sticks and cheesy biscuits?"

"Yes, of course. Now will you cheer up?"

"Mummy, take me to the stream. Just me. Please."

She considered this for a moment.

"All right. Just for a little while. Come on, then."

And suddenly, the day was beautiful once more. Cares forgotten, Thomas rushed to the stream, took off his shoes and socks this time, and paddled in the water. Mummy read and dozed. Mr. Rab picked some flowers and Hedgecock floated twigs downstream.

> *"Winter's short,*
> *Summer's long,*
> *Let's all sing*
> *A Flowering song!"*

27

warbled Mr. Rab.

"Twenty-one, twenty-two, twenty-three," Hedge-cock grunted.

At last Mummy got up, rather slowly, for it was pleasant on the warm, soft grass.

"If we're going to have our picnic tea, I'd better go and get it ready," she said.

They walked home in the sunny afternoon and Mummy went into the kitchen. The voices of Gwendolyn and Blossom on the lawn sounded just a little peevish. They were quarrelling as to which one was to be the chief princess. A day spent in each other's company had been too much, and Blossom had begun to wish that she'd gone to the stream instead of listening to a long recital of Gwendolyn's cleverness and achievements.

Thomas squatted in a far corner of the lawn and began to make a worm collection. Glorious things, worms. Daddy had told him how useful they were in the garden. He and Hedgecock tried to straighten them out to see which one was the longest. It's not easy straightening wiggly, wriggly worms but very interesting if you happen to like them, which Mr. Rab didn't.

> "*A wriggling worm*
> *Just makes me squirm*,"

he shuddered.

Thomas and Hedgecock took no notice. The worms felt cool and smooth, and there were lots of them.

"Thirty-three, thirty-four, thirty-five," Hedgecock counted.

Gwendolyn could not resist; over she came to the counting figures.

"Ooeeowh," she squealed. "How horrid. How nasty. Oh, you are a dirty, beastly little boy, aren't you, Thomas?"

He didn't reply, having just found a good cluster under the apple tree, but Gwendolyn went on.

"I've heard a lot about you. Blossom says how awful you are."

Blossom's cheeks began to go red. She was squirming inside, just like Mr. Rab, only not because of the

29

worms which she didn't mind at all. She'd realized that she much preferred Thomas to Gwendolyn, and remembered the tree-house and his anger and disappointment when he'd been shut out of the games. Gwendolyn was going on and on, as she always did when she got started on a topic.

"Fifty-four, fifty-five, fifty-six," Thomas counted. Mr. Rab sang under his breath:

> "*Gwendolyn's a silly twit,*
> *I don't like her one little bit.*"

"I should hate to have you for a brother," Gwendolyn shrilled on.

Blossom thought her voice sounded like a dentist's drill, and she half hoped that Thomas would explode in one of his furies, but feared what would happen if he did.

"Why, you don't even say hedgehog, you say hedgecock. I've heard you. A hedgecock, I ask you!" Gwendolyn twittered gaily.

Thomas looked up at her curls bobbing up and down, pale blonde curls like corkscrews. "Just like worms," he thought, and, seizing his collection, he threw them with careful aim all over her face and hair.

Mother had always had a gift for appearing at the wrong moment. Bearing a tray of food she was just in time to see and hear Gwendolyn screaming hysterically, brushing off hordes of worms.

"I'm never coming here again," she shrieked as she rushed away.

"Blossom, go after her and apologize to her. I know he won't," Mother said as she put down the tray.

"Oh Thomas, how could you? Why on earth did you?"

He stood sullen and silent, but Blossom, her face crimson, cried:

"It was her fault. He wasn't doing anything and she went on and on, saying nasty things, and laughing at Thomas because of Hedgecock."

She stopped and burst into tears.

"Well, Thomas?"

"I'm sorry—a bit."

"You don't throw worms at people, however badly they behave. Blossom, there's a box of chocolates at the top of the cupboard. Run after her and say Thomas is sorry and give her the box. Then we'll have our tea out here. It's a pity to waste it. But, Thomas, go and wash your hands. I don't share your fondness for worms."

> "Oh lovely, shiny, frabjous day
> Gwendolyn has gone away,"

carolled Mr. Rab.

"There were fifty-nine worms altogether," Hedgecock announced. "Shall I let them go?"

"Yes," they all shouted together.

Chapter Three

Blossom and Thomas had awoken early and begun on the posters requested by Tamworth Pig. Hedgecock assisted, but Mr. Rab still lay in bed, nose a-twitch, dreaming of living in a burrow with real rabbits, his favourite dream. Blossom's posters were beautiful, neatly lettered, and decorated with drawings of grapes and apples, and the hives of honey-bees. Thomas's were covered with finger marks and large wobbly letters that wandered up and down the paper. Blossom's read "Make more Food", and Thomas's "Grow more Grub". Hedgecock was doing some of his own on rather tatty torn-off scraps. "Vote for T. Pig of Baggs's Farm" he wrote. He also counted them. Blossom had done twelve, very neatly, Thomas nineteen, rather messily, and Hedgecock seven.

"I wish I hadn't got to go to school," Blossom moaned. "I'd like to deliver these to Tamworth now, not wait till four o'clock."

"That's simple," Hedgecock replied. "Don't go."

"Oh, but I must."

"Why?"

"To learn."

Hedgecock snorted. "You can read and write and

draw, now. You'll never learn to do sums any more than Mr. Rab will. And Tamworth can tell you more than anybody. He knows everything. School is Mrs. Twitchie. Ugh!"

Mr. Rab woke up in the middle of the speech, rubbing his eyes.

"What was all that about?"

"Hedgecock says it's no good going to school."

"Oh, but he's so wrong, so very wrong, as usual," Mr. Rab quavered, ignoring Hedgecock's fierce glare. "First of all, you have to learn to be good, you see. That's the most important lesson. And you can't really learn it at home, because you have to learn to mix with other people, and like them. Even the horrid ones. You see, they have just as much right to be them as you have to be you. Hedgecock and Thomas just think that what they think is right, is right, if you see what I mean. Don't hit me."

Hedgecock did hit him, and Mr. Rab cried, but he spoke on bravely.

"I know if I'd ever been to school, I wouldn't be so shy with real rabbits. I'd be able to be friends with them."

Thomas put down the posters.

"When you two have finished, she'll have to go 'cos she'll get walloped if she doesn't. Now shut up. You can come with me to take them to Tamworth."

"Don't forget to ask him about making money, he must have some ideas by now," Blossom said as they went down to eat their breakfast.

Tamworth was pleased to see them. He was running

happily around his half-acre of land, most of which was trampled down and eaten clean of grass, flowers, shoots, thistles, nettles—the lot. Pigs are wonderful at clearing ground. They often have to have rings in their snouts to stop them destroying too much, but Tamworth wasn't ringed. Mr. Baggs had considered it, but on seeing the look in Tamworth's eyes had refrained from doing so.

Thomas had brought two carrier bags with him, one containing the posters, the other some apples and potato peelings. Tamworth was pleased with the apples, but the peelings he regarded with disdain. He ate them all the same.

"Sorry to be ungracious, dear Thomas. It's just that Mrs. Baggs, that extremely mean woman, gives them to me all the time. Hardly ever do I get any proper pig food. Swill, I believe they call it. A nasty word. I do wish that people would realize that we pigs are essentially clean, fastidious animals. We suffer because of the lazy, inefficient methods of humans. Now if I were Prime Minister, it would all be changed. You see. . . ."

Thomas brought out the posters from his bag in order to stop Tamworth, who seemed likely to go on for ever.

"It's a day for people making long speeches."

Thomas himself believed in action, not words.

Tamworth examined the posters.

"Mm. Not bad. Not bad at all. Blossom's are very nice. Refined. They give tone to the whole proceeding. Those are yours, Thomas, I suppose. Well, we must be grateful for small mercies. Still, they'll do.

Hedgecock, I presume these are yours. Quite hideous, but the idea's good. I'd like them copied by Blossom, with my name in full and with a portrait of me on them—in profile."

"What's profile?" Thomas asked.

"Sideways on," Hedgecock hissed back. "Showing his snout and tail."

"Quite right, though somewhat inelegantly expressed. Perhaps our great poet Mr. Rab may pen a few rhymes in my honour and we can write them on a poster."

Mr. Rab simpered with delight and started rhyming immediately.

> *"Vote for Pig*
> *He's really big.*
> *Tamworth—er—hamworth."*

Hedgecock kicked him.

"What 'ave we got to vote for you for, anyway?" Joe said, ambling from nowhere into the morning. "'Ave we got an animals' Parliament or summat? And will it get me more oats and 'ay?"

Tamworth sat silent as though thunderstruck. At last he spoke.

"Of course, of course. Out of the mouths of hedgecocks and horses cometh wisdom. You've hit it."

He snorted three times.

"That's it. I'll be President of the Animals' Parliament. I think someone thought of something similar. George, his name was. But I shall do better—much better."

He charged three times round his ground and sat down again, breathless.

"On with the posters, Thomas. Joe, get together all the animals you can muster and tell all the pigeons, owls, sparrows and starlings—yes, especially the starlings—they're a chatty crowd—that there's a meeting in the orchard, tonight, at midnight. Spread the word."

"By the way," Thomas said, before Tamworth got too carried away, "Blossom told me to ask about the money."

"What money?"

Tamworth was occupied with a vision of himself as the chief animal of the British Isles.

"We want to get some money because Mummy and Daddy are poor."

Thomas sounded bored but it was only because he'd already explained this and he hated wasting words.

"Oh, that. Well, a little money can be earned easily, like this. Gather some wild flowers, tie a ribbon round them, put them in water—jam jars will do—and sit by the roadside and sell them. Trippers will buy them, telling their friends they picked them in the wild woods and then do quite nasty flower arrangements at home with two twigs and a piece of bark."

"I don't fancy that," Thomas said.

"Blossom and I will do it," Mr. Rab volunteered.

"Well, then, Thomas. You know Ethelberta Ever-Ready, the hen that lays so many? She has a secret nest by the old barn that isn't used any more and Mrs. Baggs, that mean woman of whom you've doubtless heard me speak, hasn't found it yet. Ethelberta keeps on laying and laying and there are dozens of eggs there. Show them by the roadside with a special poster saying 'Extra fresh eggs here in the countryside', and motorists will buy them for far more than they would pay in the shops."

"What about half as much again?" Hedgecock the mathematician asked.

"That would be excellent," Tamworth said.

"We'll do that. Good-bye. Thanks, Tamworth."

"Are you coming to the meeting?"

"No, it's too late, but I'll come and hear about it later."

"More oats and 'ay is what I'll say," Joe promised.

Tamworth was walking up and down composing speeches as they left.

They meandered through the fields for some time, then followed the ditches home, swatting nettles and flies with their sticks. Thomas stopped to cut off a stem of hedge-parsley to make a blowpipe to blow the hawthorn buds through. And out of the corner of his eye he saw a flash of red jersey on the other side of the hedge.

"Look out," he whispered to Hedgecock. "Robin Redbreast is about."

Quietly they ran along to climb the stile that led into the next field, and crouching behind the hedge were Christopher Robin and Lurcher Dench, preparing to jump him. Thomas's face was crimson, his eyes shining with excitement. He stepped to one side to avoid Christopher's mis-timed rush, putting out his foot very neatly to trip him head first into the nettle-

filled, watery ditch, There was a despairing wail from Christopher as his face encountered mud, weed, snails, nettles and the bramble.

Thomas turned to deal with Lurcher. Putting his head down, he rushed at him and butted him in the solar plexus. Lurcher fell back, winded, but not for long. Recovering his breath, he rushed forward, arms flailing like a windmill. Thomas knelt down and Lurcher fell over him. Up he jumped, aiming kicks at Thomas's shins and pulling his sweater so hard that the seams parted down one side.

Hedgecock yelled: "Come on, Thomas. Bash him."

Lurcher kicked him out of the way. Then Thomas went berserk. He charged at Lurcher, hitting left to the head, right to the body and left to the nose, which was bleeding as Lurcher stumbled away. He didn't cry. But by now, Christopher Robin had emerged even spottier from the nettles, shouting unprintable words about what he was going to do to Thomas, who hit him firmly in one eye. Mrs. Baggs's boy departed howling.

"Come on," Thomas said. "Stop shivering, Mr. Rab. I'm all right."

"Yes, we won," Hedgecock said.

"Of course we did, we always shall, but I wonder what Mummy will say. She'll never believe I didn't start it."

She didn't.

He said to Tamworth Pig later that day as he sat curled up beside him with Num covering them both:

"Grown-ups are unfair, Tamworth."

"Something that you have to learn, Thomas, is the terrible injustice of life. Even you and I, deserving and worthy as we are, cannot win all the time."

Chapter Four

———————— * ————————

Whitsuntide holidays had come round and Blossom was to have a week at home. Money-making plans could be put into operation, but first Tamworth must be visited to see if he needed any further assistance in his campaign for "Grow more Grub but Eat less Meat".

Blossom had finished twenty "Vote for Tamworth Pig—He's really Big" posters. He looked most handsome in profile with his long snout and curling tail. They took these along with several offerings for Tamworth's enormous appetite. Hedgecock also hopefully took a chessboard. He was growing a little tired of posters and campaigns and wished he had never started the idea. Previously he had enjoyed a game of chess with Tamworth, but now the pig always seemed too busy.

Tamworth was trotting up and down under the damson tree.

"We've held our meeting," he said. "We've sent out the posters and animals are showing great interest. We've got in touch with farms over all the county. If I can get enough support to be elected President of the Animals' Parliament I shall approach the Minister of Agriculture and put our case before him."

"But how will you get to see him?" Blossom asked, practical as ever. "A pig can't walk into the Houses of Parliament."

Mr. Rab choked back a giggle as Tamworth frowned on him.

"No, I don't especially wish to go to London. I don't think I should care for the traffic. But we shall ask the Minister to come here. He's always willing to visit farms."

"Won't you play chess, instead?" Hedgecock asked. "The black knight is going quite green from not being used."

"I may play games again in the future, but, at present, I must dedicate myself to the Cause."

"You're really keen, aren't you, Tamworth?"

"There's not much point in doing anything unless you put your heart and soul into it. By the way, Jasper, that particularly black-hearted stallion, is putting his heart and soul into opposing me, aided and abetted by the miserable cur, Rover, the dog. We shall have to do something about them."

He distributed his great weight down in the most comfortable position.

"Good-bye. Time for my morning snooze."

He drifted off to sleep, a red-gold heap under the damson tree.

"Let's visit Ethelberta's nest and see if we can get some eggs to sell," Thomas said.

"You do that while I get my flower stall ready," Blossom said. "We'd better not choose a place too near home or Mummy will find out."

The next day was perfect, and, of the cars that streamed along the road, many stopped to buy "Pretty

Flowers", and "Fresher than Fresh Eggs from the Country". By evening they'd taken two pounds, according to Hedgecock, who kept the account.

They returned home flushed with pride, and hid the money in a tin at the bottom of Thomas's wardrobe.

"They're up to something," Mummy said, late that night.

Daddy put down his paper.

"What makes you think so?"

"They're so quiet. Something's up."

"If they are we'll soon find out. Thomas will do something he shouldn't and give the show away."

The weather remained sunny and the children had another good day. Wild flowers were blooming everywhere, and Ethelberta was still laying eggs at a great rate, so they had plenty of produce to sell. In all, the takings totalled four pounds and they sat in Thomas's room and discussed what they were going to do with the money. Blossom wrote down the final decision, which went like this.

> One pound to Tamworth Pig for the Fund.
> One pound to starving children.

"Better send that to Oxfam," Blossom had said.

> One pound to Mummy and Daddy as a present.
> One pound to spend on . . .

"Sweets, chocolates, crisps, ice-cream, lemonade," they all cried together.

Heavy footsteps sounded on the stairs.

"It's Daddy," Blossom whispered. "Hide the tin."

A hasty scuffle followed and Blossom shoved the tin under the pillow as the door opened to reveal both Mummy and Daddy.

"Mrs. Baggs has just called. She says you've been taking their eggs to sell at the roadside. Gwendolyn Twitchie told her."

"She would," Thomas muttered.

"Is this true?" Daddy asked in a stern voice.

"They're Ethelberta's eggs, not Mrs. Baggs's."

"Ethelberta belongs to Mrs. Baggs and so do her eggs. Anyway, Mrs. Baggs was obviously telling the truth. Stop crying, Blossom, and tell me how much money you got for them."

They brought out the tin from under the pillow and made a hasty calculation, helped by Hedgecock. Blossom's tears fell all over the money, damping a very beautiful new pound note.

"We got two pounds for the eggs and two pounds for the wild flowers."

"Oh, so you've been selling wild flowers too?"

"Yes," Blossom howled. "We didn't think it was wrong. We only wanted to make some money 'cos we're so poor. We were going to give some to you."

Daddy and Mummy looked at one another.

"We're not so poor that you have to take other people's eggs and sell them. Give the money to me," Daddy said.

"You can keep the flower money," Mummy said. "But the rest must go to Mrs. Baggs."

"That horrible mean woman," Thomas muttered. "I bet she won't give any of it to Tamworth."

45

"What's that, Thomas?"

"Nothing."

"Don't mumble, boy. And Blossom, don't sell too many flowers. Much of the countryside is being ruined by people picking too many flowers. At this rate there'll be none left."

Mummy and Daddy went downstairs with the tin. The little band sat in a miserable heap on the bed.

"Never mind, we've still got two pounds left," Mr. Rab said.

"Yes, but it doesn't feel the same," Blossom wailed. "It doesn't feel nice any more."

"Two pound notes must feel nice, only four pounds felt better," Hedgecock growled. "More is always better than less."

"More school isn't better than less school," Thomas said.

"I think Mr. Rab's right," Blossom said. "We've still got a pound for Tamworth and a pound for ourselves."

Chapter Five

---------------*------------------

Uncle Jeff and Aunt Cynthia came for a holiday. Blossom loved them, but Thomas detested them. Mummy never seemed very cheery either during their visit, perhaps because she was always in the kitchen, cooking. Uncle Jeff liked lots of food. He was Daddy's brother and they laughed a lot together.

There were lots of people detested by Thomas, but on his special list of hates, Mrs. Baggs came first, Gwendolyn Twitchie second, Christopher Robin Baggs third and Aunt Cynthia fourth.

She was unusually tall and thin with elongated bones sticking out in all directions, and fuzzy, pink hair like candy floss. She was very proud of her hair and was always washing it, after which she would walk round in green plastic rollers looking like a creature from outer space. Her finger-nails were long, polished and pointed like daggers and almost as dangerous. She piled her dressing-table with jars and perfumes and talcum powder and bottles and brushes. When Thomas was very young, about four, he had crept into her room and covered himself with cream and powder and then drawn faces all over the mirror with lipstick and mascara. He thought it looked very pretty, but no one

47

agreed with this idea. Aunt Cynthia had never liked him after that, not that she'd ever been very fond of him, anyway.

"Nasty, rude, spoilt little boy," she squeaked to Uncle Jeff.

Every year Thomas hoped she wouldn't come, but she always did, and he would watch her waggling walk and try not to listen to her high-pitched, niminy-piminy voice and think how nasty she was, especially when Blossom, who always copied other people's mannerisms, started to waggle and squeak too.

"It's really horrible," he said to Hedgecock.

Everyone else had gone shopping and they were playing with the green rollers, which they'd found in a polythene bag on the mantelpiece. They'd made them into forts, pretended they were soldiers, or, by putting them on their spiky sides, turned them into barbed-wire barricades. They arranged them in fives and eights, counting them happily. There were thirty-seven.

"A peculiar number," Hedgecock said. "There's always something over when you put it into twos or threes or fives or anything. There's others like it: thirteen or nineteen fr'instance. They ought to have a special name. Tamworth will know what it is."

They arranged them in a pattern on the flat top of the guard that was always bolted round the fire. Aunt Cynthia felt the cold, so there were constant hot fires despite the warm weather.

They went out into the garden. Time passed and then there came an appalling scream from the house.

Thomas sat back on his heels, listening with interest. Something was obviously going on.

Aunt Cynthia shot out of the door wailing like a cat with its tail trapped, and she bore down on Thomas.

"I'm going to slaughter you. I'm going to give you the hiding of a lifetime, you dreadful boy!"

Thomas did not stop to reason why. He leapt to his feet and fled as fast as he could go with Aunt Cynthia hot on his heels. But his legs were much shorter than her long ones, and in desperation he headed for Tamworth Pig, who was sitting in his favourite place under the damson tree.

"I shall catch you," Aunt Cynthia cried. "Don't think you can get away."

"Save me," Thomas panted as he scrambled on to the golden back.

Always ready to answer a cry for help, Tamworth heaved himself on to his trotters and Thomas held on for dear life. He pawed the ground, then charged full tilt with all his weight behind him at the rapidly approaching aunt. Her screams of rage changed into a different key as the Pig of Pigs hurtled towards her with Thomas clutching the furry ears. She spun around and, if anything, ran even faster back to home and safety.

"Horrible children and mad animals," she cried down on to Mummy's shoulder, which wasn't easy as she was much taller than Mummy, who finally got her off to bed with an aspirin.

Having settled the sorrowing aunt, she went to fetch

Thomas, who was now hiding between Tamworth and the damson tree, pretending not to be there.

"Tamworth," she remarked politely, handing him a pear, as he was an old friend of hers, "justice has to be done. Thomas must come home."

"Yes, I know, yet I am strangely reluctant to part with my young friend. Come out, Thomas."

Thomas lifted an unhappy face from behind the broad and sheltering back.

"I don't know what I'm supposed to have done."

"Just come in and I'll show you."

Thomas crept out slowly, slipped his hand into Mummy's and they went off together.

"Think of the Cause," Tamworth called after them. "Be brave, Thomas."

Thomas felt anything but brave. Mummy led him

50

to the fireguard, where lots of green blobs had spread, while others hung in dangling ringlets.

"Oh, the curlers melted."

"Yes," Daddy said, appearing from nowhere as he so often did. "When I've spanked you, you can go and apologize to Aunt Cynthia. Then, tomorrow, you can buy her some more with your pocket money."

Funnily enough, it wasn't a severe spanking, not one of Daddy's mightier efforts. He even seemed to be laughing a little. Perhaps he didn't like curlers either. Saying sorry was hard as it always is, especially to Aunt Cynthia. But it must have worked for she decided to stay a bit longer after all. She'd been packing her case when Mummy pushed him into the bedroom to make his speech.

"Just think," he said in bed that night. "If I'd refused to say sorry, she might have gone by now."

"Let's forget her," Hedgecock replied. "I was talking to Tamworth after you'd gone and he said those peculiar numbers like thirty-seven are called Prime numbers. Like Prime Pork, I said. Then he went all sulky and wouldn't talk to me."

"He hates you to mention pork or bacon or sausages," Mr. Rab said. "It makes him very sad. You are stupid, Hedgecock."

Hedgecock bashed Mr. Rab several times for that remark, but finally they all settled down to sleep.

Chapter Six

————————————*————————————

Uncle Jeff was quite a different shape from his wife, being tubby and bald, with a huge ginger moustache. He laughed a lot. He tickled Blossom under the chin and told her she was a smasher.

"That's right," Hedgecock muttered. "She's always breaking things."

Uncle Jeff sang as he helped with the washing up, and he sang as he came back from the "Duck and Dragon" with Daddy late at night. Daddy also sang, reported Mr. Rab, who never slept very soundly, unlike Hedgecock, who snored the dark away.

Blossom loved Uncle Jeff. She sat on his knee, wriggling and giggling as he asked:

"What key won't open a door?"

Blossom didn't know.

"A donkey, of course," he roared and they both fell on the floor with laughter. Cherry Blossom he called her.

He was very jolly with Thomas for three or four days, laughed and sang and told jokes, while his nephew remained unsmiling and expressionless, just staring at him. Actually he didn't think much of the jokes or the singing, but the ginger moustache he found fascinating.

"There's something peculiar about that boy of yours," Uncle Jeff said to Mummy, who was ironing. "I can't get on with him at all. He just sits and stares. Are you sure there's nothing wrong with him?"

"He isn't good with people," Mummy said, ironing fiercely and scorching something. "Oh bother." She sounded cross.

"I'm not people. After all, we come here every year and he never even says hello to me."

"Hello," Thomas said.

"Well, at least he understands what I say. I was beginning to wonder if he was quite right in the head."

Mummy banged down the iron.

"Thomas is quite clever and he understands everything you say."

"I wonder if they'll have a row," Mr. Rab whispered to Hedgecock.

They were sitting under the table waiting for Thomas to start a game but he was too busy gazing at the ginger moustache.

"I hope so."

Hedgecock loved rows, but, at that moment, Blossom burst in, her brown eyes shining, and flung herself at Uncle Jeff.

"Tell me a story," she cried.

"Did I tell you about the time I had to come down by parachute over enemy territory?"

"Hundreds of times," Daddy said, coming in for the paper and retreating with it hastily.

"No, he hasn't. Please tell me, Uncle Jeff. I want to hear."

"Well, I was in the Army, and one day a small group of us had to be transported to another unit by aeroplane. The weather was bad and we went off course, and, suddenly, this fighter appeared out of nowhere—guns firing—rat-tat-tat-tat. . . ."

Thomas came even nearer to watch the moustache.

"Were you frightened?" breathed Blossom.

"Scared stiff. They hit us and we were told to jump. . . ."

"From up in the air?"

"Yes. I was terrified the parachute wouldn't open."

"But it did," Thomas spoke up. "Or you'd have been all smashed up dead. Splattered all over the ground."

"Don't go on," Uncle Jeff said, looking pained.

"Where did you land?"

"In enemy territory. But a farmer hid me on his farm, smuggled me to the coast and I got a boat for England."

"Oh, you were brave."

Blossom's eyes were starry.

"Parachutes are nice things, like big balloons or umbrellas. Like big balloons or umbrellas," Thomas went on muttering to himself.

Next day he found a ladder and put it up to an outhouse roof. He was quiet and careful, as he didn't wish to be caught. Mr. Rab didn't like this new game at all for he was afraid of heights. After climbing up and down once or twice, Thomas fetched Blossom. She went up cheerfully, and they sat on the roof. Then Thomas crawled up to the chimney and produced two umbrellas from behind it, one a beautiful red and yellow one shaped like a pagoda, the other old and shabby.

Blossom looked horrified.

"What are you doing with those? That's Mummy's new one."

"Shan't hurt them. They're going to be our parachutes. We open them and jump off the roof. You can have the pretty one."

"Oh no, not me."

"It's quite safe. Look, Num's lying on the periwinkle bed to catch us."

Blossom looked down on the grey form of Num spread out apparently hundreds of feet below.

"No, I won't. I won't!"

She stood up, nearly fell off, and sat down again, hastily.

Thomas pushed his face close to hers, his eyes a hard blue stare.

"You took money from Mummy's purse. If you don't jump, I shall tell her."

"I gave some to you. Then I was sorry. I put it all back later and I never did it again."

Blossom cried in anguish, her face red, rocking noisily to and fro in her grief. Mr. Rab shut his eyes. He couldn't bear to look.

"She'll still be angry and sad, so jump."

"Jump," echoed Hedgecock.

"Don't," wept Mr. Rab.

"We'll hold umbrellas in one hand and each other's hands with the other," Thomas said.

Sad and tearstained, Blossom opened the glorious new umbrella. Thomas opened Daddy's greenish-black one. They stood up together and Blossom closed her eyes tight.

"I'm frightened," Mr. Rab wailed.

"Don't be silly. It's only a little jump," Hedgecock growled.

At that moment Mummy came round the corner just in time to see two figures leaping off the roof, one howling miserably. She saw her best umbrella blow inside out, and Blossom miss the soft comfort of Num and the periwinkle bed to fall heavily, her head striking a stone. She lay still, her face as white as it had been red earlier.

"Oh, oh," Mr. Rab shrieked.

"Trouble, trouble, trouble," Hedgecock groaned.

Blossom was not badly hurt, though she had to stay in bed for a few days. This time, Thomas wasn't spanked, but Mummy and Daddy talked long and seriously to him, and found out just why she had jumped when she was so afraid. Thomas promised to be a better boy. He really meant it, this time. In bed, at last, he held Num tightly and said:

"You were supposed to catch her too, Num."

"It's only your Num. It can't look after everyone," Mr. Rab said.

"Let's buy Blossom some sweets," Hedgecock suggested, which was a great concession for him as he was a mean animal.

Mr. Rab cheered up immediately.

"I'll write her a poem."

"Oh, no, there's no need to go that far," Hedgecock said, but Mr. Rab was away.

"Blossom high up on the roof,
 Terrified was she,
 Closed her eyes and then she fell
 Like a falling blossom from a tree."

"Oh, lumme, that's worse than usual," Hedgecock said and retired to the foot of the bed to count squares.

"I admit it's not very good, but it was on the spur of the moment."

Mr. Rab was always hurt by unkind remarks about his poems.

"Sing a bedtime song," Thomas whispered.

Mr. Rab sang, but for once its magic did not work and Thomas lay awake for a long time thinking of the difficulties of being a better boy until he too fell asleep to the gentle sound of Mr. Rab's snuffles and the monotonous whirring of Hedgecock's snores.

Chapter Seven

---*---

Thomas spent a miserable time while Blossom was in bed. He watched trays being carried up to her room, he saw the doctor running brightly up and down the stairs and Aunt Cynthia creeping about on the very tipmost of tiptoes, with finger ever at her lips motioning silence to everyone, especially him. Worst of all, Mummy had a worried, far-away look on her face which made it very difficult to go near her. She was always cooking, not making cakes or pies or rolling glorious strips of pastry, but simmering thin soups and beating up egg yolks. Whenever he dared to enter the kitchen he was immediately sent out to play. He wanted to go in and see Blossom and no one would let him, and he began to get the idea that she would die and it would all be his fault. Aunt Cynthia made it much worse.

"It's funny how such a little boy can cause such a lot of trouble," she shrilled. "Here you are, the smallest, the least of all of us, the last and youngest in the family and you cause more work and worry than the rest put together. I know what I'd do with you if I were your mother—I'd treat you like the nasty little baby you are, smack you hard, and send you to bed for a week, like poor, dear, sweet Blossom. The trouble with you is that you think you're important, whereas you come last in everything, or should do."

"Oh, do shut up, Cynthia," Uncle Jeff said, putting down his book. "Leave the boy alone."

He quite liked Thomas these days after the umbrella incident.

The boy in question wandered drearily away to find Tamworth Pig, who was fast asleep under his favourite tree. He put his head on the gently heaving fat form and felt comforted.

He and Hedgecock dozed off, but Mr. Rab stayed awake, nose and paws a-twitch. Minutes ticked slowly past, afternoon fashion. At last there was a convulsive heave as if someone were stirring a giant Christmas pudding. Tamworth was waking up. He rolled from side to side, then stood up abruptly, shaking his ears. Thomas and Hedgecock rolled over like a couple of ping-pong balls off a table, rubbed their eyes and were awake.

When they had finished yawning Tamworth said:

"I must tell you that we're having a special meeting tonight to vote Jasper or me as President. Will you come, this time? We need help to count the votes."

"Yes, I'll come," Hedgecock said. "I like counting."

"Well, Barry McKenzie Goat has offered to wait outside your house and bring you to the meeting."

"I'll come," Thomas said. "But Blossom can't. Oh, Tamworth, she isn't going to die, is she?"

"Of course not. What a silly idea. She'll live to be a hundred. Now, off you go, I've got to make up my speeches. Oh, Thomas, give my regards to Aunt Cynthia. She looked so funny when last I saw her."

He guffawed, and Thomas too began to smile, until he was bellowing with laughter as well. Soon they were all helpless with mirth under the damson tree.

When they arrived home, Mummy said:

"Blossom's asking to see you. You can go up and play after tea."

Sunlight exploded inside Thomas. He looked around, loving everyone.

"Hello, Uncle Jeff. Hallo, Aunt Cynthia. I'm glad you came to stay."

Uncle Jeff snorted into his teacup, blowing tea everywhere, and even Aunt Cynthia smiled.

Blossom had a marvellously huge bandage round her head. Mr. Rab was jealous so she made one for him as well. They sat on her bed while she read to

them from *The Wind in the Willows*. Then they acted it. Hedgecock was Badger, Blossom was Ratty, Mr. Rab was Mole and Thomas was Toad, of course.

After a while, Blossom felt tired, so Mummy took Thomas to bed, where he lay determined to stay awake for the meeting.

Chapter Eight

———————————✳———————————

Thomas awoke with a start, for he had fallen asleep after all. He drew back the curtains and found it was already dark outside. He pulled a thick sweater and jeans over his pyjamas, and then put on his plimsolls so that he could move quietly. He draped Num around his neck, woke up the twitching Mr. Rab and the snoring Hedgecock, and they cautiously made their way downstairs, past Mummy's and Daddy's room where a light still showed under the door, and through the kitchen, silent but for the ticking of the clock. They pulled back the bolt, which made a grinding noise, and then out into the garden. It was so quiet that Thomas almost turned back but then he saw Barry McKenzie Goat's head peering over the wall, so he climbed over and put his hand on the hairy side.

"Come on, they're nearly ready to begin."

They hurried through the wet grass and into the orchard. There, by the light of flickering lanterns, sat cows, horses, sheep, pigs, goats, hens, turkeys, cats, ducks and dogs. There were even some rats and mice scurrying about and owls hooted in the trees.

Tamworth was seated under the damson tree, a magnificent sight in the lantern glow. On one side was

Joe the Shire Horse and Barry McKenzie Goat led
Thomas to the other. The animals formed a great
circle with Tamworth and Jasper, the stallion, at
opposite ends of the diameter. Joe was Chairman, but
was not very conspicuous. As Barry and Thomas took
their places, Jasper was speaking in a rolling neigh.

"This idea of Tamworth's is absolutely worthless,
useless and impractical. We shall never persuade our
farming friends to sell less meat. Farmers make their
money from selling animals for meat. We must just
put up with this."

"Hear, hear," Rover barked.

He was a sheepdog and an especial favourite of Mrs.
Baggs.

Tamworth rose to his trotters.

"Brother animals, brothers all," he cried. "We must remember that my black and spirited opponent here has hardly the same outlook as the rest of us, or most of us. If there is a chance that Brother Jasper may end up inside a dog-meat tin, that day is long distant, and as for our barking friend here, no one would ever contemplate eating him, a fact which I do not find at all surprising. But the rest of us tastier brothers are liable to be cut down in our prime, oh horrible word, at any time. However, this is only one point from my campaign. The main thing is that we must get the country to grow more food. If you support me in this and elect me as your President, I shall send an invitation to our Minister at the Houses of Parliament so that he may visit us and learn about our ideas."

"Hear, hear," Thomas shouted, quite carried away. "Grow more grub!"

Jasper turned to Rover.

"I do not think this young human should be present at a meeting of animals."

He glared with wild, rolling eyes at Thomas, who wrapped Num around himself and said:

"I am always on Tamworth's side——"

"On his back," Hedgecock hissed.

"—even if it does mean no roast ever."

It was easy for him. He hated roast. Poor Blossom would miss her Sunday dinner sadly if Tamworth had his way.

Jasper continued.

"Mr. Chairman, I wish to ask why this human is present tonight. I wish to object."

"Brother Thomas and Brother 'edgecock are 'ere to count votes. They don't 'ave any say theirselves. Objection over-ruled."

Tamworth had taught Joe "objection over-ruled" earlier in the day.

Barry McKenzie Goat stood up.

"I should like to propose Brother Tamworth as President of the Animals' Union, whose aim is to encourage more food growing in England for the good and happiness of all, including us animals."

He sat down again, and Joe spoke.

"Does anyone second this?"

Fanny Cow and Ethelberta Ever-Ready stepped forward.

"Proposal carried," Thomas said cheerfully.

Then Rover spoke.

"I propose Brother Jasper, the Black Stallion, as President of Follow the Farmers League, whose aim is to keep things exactly as they are."

Joe asked for a seconder and Rufus Pony and Pussy Cat stepped forward.

"Proposal carried. Will you please put up paw, 'oof, wing or claw to cast your vote? Brothers 'edgecock and Thomas, will you count for us?"

They would never have managed the counting without Hedgecock. With beady eyes a-glitter at such a task, he counted and counted, aided by Thomas.

"It's ninety-six votes to ninety-six votes for each candidate," he panted at last.

"A draw," the cows mooed. "What happens now?"

Tamworth spoke to Joe, who then stood up.

67

"Has Chairman, I 'ave the casting vote."

Everybody waited.

"I cast me Chairman's vote for Tamworth Pig!"

There was suddenly such a chorus of cheers, boos, neighs, moos, clucks, gobbles, squeals, roars, and howls that the lights all went on at Baggs's Farm.

"Quiet," Tamworth said, and they obeyed.

"Thank you for your confidence in me. I am deeply honoured. Now we must go home silently, lest there is trouble."

The animals melted quietly away into the shadows. Lanterns went out. Thomas felt very tired and he just wanted to curl up in Num and sleep under the damson tree, but Tamworth pushed him with his snout.

"Come on. Get on my back and I'll take you home."

He lowered himself and somehow Thomas scrambled on, and they went home. All the lights in the house were out and it was very dark.

"Thank you for your help," Tamworth said.

"That's all right, dear old Tamworth," Thomas murmured.

He had to be helped over the garden wall, and he tottered up the path holding Hedgecock and Mr. Rab. Luckily the kitchen door was still unbolted and at last he tumbled into bed.

He got up the next morning very late.

"I wonder why you're so sleepy," Mummy said. "But there was a lot of noise in the night. Animals, I think. Perhaps it kept you awake?"

"Yes, it did," Thomas agreed.

Chapter Nine

———————————*———————————

Blossom wrote out an invitation to the Minister to visit Tamworth Pig in his role of President of the Animals' Union. His campaign for growing more food was becoming more and more widely known now, and he had received a deputation from the Vegetarian League, who were most interested in his idea of eating less meat. A very handsome photograph of Tamworth seated under the damson tree appeared in the *Vegetarian Times* and Blossom cut it out and pinned it up in the Pig House, which Tamworth refused to have called a sty. "My home is not a spot on someone's eye," he declared.

In due course, the Minister's secretary wrote back to say that the Minister was very busy at present, but that he hoped to visit Baggs's Farm during the next month, and with this Tamworth had to be satisfied. He passed his time improving and decorating Pig House, and in interviewing animals who had any complaints or problems. Mr. and Mrs. Baggs remained quiet, apparently unaware of the activity going on in their orchard.

The weather continued wet and unpleasant, an English summer at its worst, but Blossom did not mind this too much because she had another interest. The Vicar's wife, new to the district and full of enthusiasm, was organizing a play to be held in the Church Hall. Blossom was to be a bear and she went around reciting her lines non-stop.

The Vicar's wife visited Mummy to see if she could help with the costumes, which she agreed to do. When the visiting lady was about to leave, having partaken of tea, six sandwiches and four cakes, she said:

"Oh, by the way, I believe you have another child as well as Blossom. Doesn't he go to school or Sunday school?"

"Well, he was ill rather a lot, so he's not going to school again till September."

"Doesn't he go to Sunday school?"

Thomas's mother didn't feel like explaining that he behaved so badly that the previous Vicar's wife had asked her not to send him any more.

"No," was all she said.

"I saw him the other day and I thought what a nice boy he looked and what a beautiful angel he'd make in the play."

"Oh, no," Mummy's voice trembled. "I don't think he'd make a good angel."

"I'm sure he'll be all right. It will be good for him. He's probably shy, and acting and singing will bring him out. Children love dressing up."

"He's a very awkward boy."

The Vicar's wife laughed.

"Nonsense, he'll be as good as gold, I'm sure. Just send him with Blossom to the rehearsal on Wednesday.

Oh, and tell him" (she wagged a forefinger) "there's a wee prize for every child taking part."

Strangely enough Thomas was quite keen, but Blossom was furious.

"I'm fed up. Oh, Mum, why did you say he could be in it? He'll spoil it. I know he'll spoil it. He always does."

"Well, perhaps he'll be good this time, dear. After all he's older now. Let's give him a chance. Be fair."

"It isn't a case of being fair. He always spoils things like this. He won't fit in with the others. He's all right with animals, but he's terrible with people. I don't know why you agreed."

"Well, honestly, I never thought he'd want to be an angel."

"It's the prize. They say it's going to be a box of chocolates and he wants one."

"Let's see how he is at the first rehearsal, anyway, Blossom. Then we can decide."

"Humph," Blossom snorted.

They returned home from the rehearsal quite late, hand in hand, eyes shining.

"Mummy, Daddy, Thomas was really good."

"I am pleased," Mummy said.

"He's chief angel."

"This I shall have to see," Daddy said.

"I was very good," the chief angel announced. "And I want four slices of toast."

"Please," Mummy and Daddy said together, automatically.

"Please," the chief angel acknowledged graciously.

Days passed. Thomas attended rehearsals, behaving beautifully. He was fitted out with a long, white robe, two tinselly wings and a halo, and spent a long time in front of mirrors, admiring himself. Blossom had a furry coat with ears and paws. She grew very nervous as the great day approached.

"I do hope I get everything right. I'm so scared," she repeated over and over again.

"I am a very good angel and I shall eat my box of chocolates all to myself," Thomas stated.

"Greedy pig," Blossom shouted.

"Don't insult me and Tamworth," Thomas roared. He smote her several times and she fled howling.

The evening of the play arrived at last, and the children left early to be dressed and made up. By the time their parents came in, the church hall was filling rapidly, the orchestra, consisting of six recorders, two violins and a piano, was warming up unsteadily and the choir were filing into their seats.

The Vicar's wife could be seen rushing hither and thither. This was her first effort and she very much wanted it to be a success. A feeling of excitement grew with the shrilling of the recorders. The curtain went up at last to reveal a glade where a number of little bears were running about. Mummy's loving eye soon picked out Blossom, a rather plumper bear than the others. She said her lines clearly and correctly. Mummy beamed and Daddy mumbled behind his hand:

"I told you she'd be all right."

They sat back and waited for Thomas to come on.

He was one of several angels due to appear with St. Francis when he was blessing the animals. St. Francis, a portly, majestic figure in his brown sack, stood with hand outstretched over the little bears. Hand outstretched he waited . . . and waited. . . . Now was time for the angels, led by their chief, to enter from the wings and dance round the newly blessed animals, while the school orchestra burst into heavenly music and the school choir into divine song. The pianist struck the opening chords, then, like St. Francis he waited and waited . . . and struck the chord again, and waited.

From behind the scenery could be heard the ever-increasing noise of an argument. Mummy clutched Daddy's arm and one of the bears on the stage began to shuffle nervously. There was a scuffling sound and straight through the middle of the back curtains shot a strange figure. A white robe hitched around its neck half covered a red jersey, a tinsel halo hung from one ear and it seemed to be trying to pull off the wings attached to its back.

"I want my box of chocolates," the apparition shouted in a very loud voice. "I don't want a silly old book. I want a box of chocolates."

"Oh no," Daddy groaned as he battled to get to his feet, hampered by gloves, programmes, umbrellas and being in the middle of a row.

An arm, that of the Vicar's wife, came through the curtains and tried to pull back the figure.

"Come along now, do. Don't make such a scene. You're spoiling the play."

Thomas turned a look of sheer, righteous fury on her.

"You've spoilt it, you mean. You said we was goin'
to get a box of chocolates and all I've got is a mouldy
old book of fairy stories. It's your fault."

The audience was getting restive. Daddy had
managed to reach the end of the row. Shouts of: "Get

74

on with the play!", "Send him off!", "Shut up!", "Scotland for ever!", "Send for Tamworth Pig," boos and cheers went up.

One of the small bears ran down the stage steps sobbing dreadfully.

"I knew he would spoil it. I told and told everybody. Now will you believe me?"

Thomas stood in the centre of the stage still shouting. "Give me my box of chocolates, then I'll be an angel."

Two bears started to fight. The Vicar's wife, now struggling with Thomas, seemed to be in tears.

Daddy arrived on the stage at last, picked up the reluctant angel, still speaking loudly about his chocolates, and carried him under one arm down the gangway to the back of the hall and outside.

Above the din could be heard Lurcher Dench yelling: "Hooray for Measle Bug."

Mummy collected the weeping Blossom.

"Do you have to let us down all the time?" Daddy asked as they drove home.

"But," Thomas said, "she said she was going to give us . . ."

"We know," joined in the others, "a box of chocolates."

Thomas's voice rose above all opposition.

"She's a silly, stupid lady, that one. And that's the last time I'll be an angel."

"How right you are," Daddy replied.

Up in bed Thomas greeted Mr. Rab, Hedgecock and Num lovingly. They had been neglected of late.

"You're all right but people are stupid."

"Did you get the chocolates?" Hedgecock asked.

"Course not. Grown-ups! Huh! They always let you down. Sing the good-night song, Mr. Rab. I shall never act again."

Chapter Ten

---------------------------------- * ----------------------------------

On Baggs's Farm all was excitement. The Minister was coming! Reporters and animals were crowding into the farm. The Baggses themselves had been informed by the Minister's Secretary the previous morning and Farmer Baggs had spent the day in feverish activity, ordering gaps to be filled, gates to be repaired and extra food and vitamins for all the animals so that they would look their very best. Mrs. Baggs cleaned the house from top to bottom, dressed her dairy maids in new nylon overalls and bought herself a dress with purple flowers on it. Tamworth had an extra bucketful of food in his trough, about which he was both amused and grateful.

"I wish the Minister came every day," he said.

He'd been checking Pig House to see that it looked especially neat and tidy, and Blossom brushed him all over, which he loved. Then Thomas scratched his back for half an hour.

"I do love to be clean and well turned out," he remarked, looking at himself in Pig House mirror. "I wish people would realize this. It's not that I'm as fussy as a cat. Indeed, I'd hate to be as pernickety as some cats. But I'm cleaner than a dog, for instance. I don't get fleas."

"You haven't got much to get fleas in," Thomas pointed out, looking at the spaces between the bristles.

"Don't be impertinent, Thomas."

Tamworth flipped his ears, for he was just a bit nervous and irritable.

"It's like before my birthday," Blossom said. "I just can't wait."

"But you'll just have to," Thomas replied.

"Tell us a story, Tamworth, to pass the time."

So Tamworth told them about the Greeks whom Circe the enchantress had changed into pigs, and how Odysseus, their wily leader, landed on her isle but was saved by the god Mercury, who gave him a plant to withstand her spells.

Then he told them about St. Anthony, who had a pig that he led about with a bell round its neck.

"There's a stained-glass window somewhere, showing this handsome pig," Tamworth said. "One day when St. Anthony was in Spain, he was asked to heal the King's son, but when he heard that a sow in the town had a lame and blind piglet, he healed it first before going to cure the Prince."

"He knew what was important," Thomas said.

Crowds were gathering round the farm. Photographers and reporters were wandering hither and thither. People from the Vegetarian Society had arrived by now and were walking up and down holding banners. Barry McKenzie and Joe took up their positions outside Pig House and Ethelberta was perched on the roof. Jasper and Rover were at the farmhouse, standing as quietly as Mr. and Mrs. Baggs were running up and down. Christopher Robin, arrayed in his best suit and a hideous pair of pink socks, sat moodily on the doorstep. He found it all a great bore, except that he, like Blossom, had a day's holiday from school. Gwendolyn had scarlatina, which was a good thing for everyone, except, possibly, Gwendolyn. Mummy was there with the Vicar's wife, but Daddy had refused to come, for crowds weren't in his line at all.

"Give my regards to Tamworth," he said.

Hedgecock and Mr. Rab, full of excitement, kept scuttling in and out of Pig House, and getting in Joe's way. He was so very large and always afraid of putting his huge hoofs down on something or someone small.

The warm afternoon and its crowd waited.

"It's five to three. He'll be here in a minute," Blossom said.

"Five minutes," Hedgecock corrected, accurate as ever.

A procession of cars appeared. He was early. The photographers pressed forward. A few voices called "Hurray", and the school orchestra struck up a raggedy note on six recorders, a flute and the drum, as the Minister alighted from his Rolls-Royce Silver Cloud.

He shook the hands of Mr. and Mrs. Baggs, patted Christopher's head and asked them to lead him on a tour of the farm, so off they went with a trail of people following, ruining Mrs. Baggs's herbaceous borders.

"What a wonderful place," he exclaimed, eyes darting everywhere over barns, animals, haystacks, milking equipment and machinery. "Beautifully kept. You are a credit to our country, Farmer er . . . er . . . er . . ."

"Baggs," his secretary whispered from behind, as he busily scribbled down notes in a little black book.

"Farmer Baggs," the Minister continued smoothly. "These fields, the hay, the wheat. . . ." Here he climbed on a gate to look down over the pleasant countryside. "It's wonderful to see the results of such industry and efficiency."

Mr. Baggs smiled broadly. He was a kind man and a good farmer. It was his wife whom nobody could bear. She stood screwing up her grey hair with her fingers.

"And now may I meet our famous Tamworth Pig, whose invitation brought me here?"

Mr. Baggs beamed. "Of course," he said as he led the way. "We're right proud of him, you know. He gets some funny ideas, he do, but there's no pig like Tamworth."

Mrs. Baggs glared out of her small, blue, beady eyes.

Tamworth was waiting, his huge beautiful shape standing firmly on his four neat little trotters. On one side was Joe, on the other Barry McKenzie with Blossom and Thomas, holding Hedgecock with Mr. Rab at his feet. Pig House was resplendent in posters, photographs of Tamworth, drawings by Blossom and pictures of food, all kinds of food except meat.

"Ah, Tamworth Pig, I presume," the Minister said, proffering his hand.

"I am deeply honoured, brother," Tamworth said

lifting a trotter. "With your permission, I should like to speak to you alone."

The Minister frowned slightly.

"It's somewhat unusual," he said. "But then, this is rather a special case. Let us go into your—er—sty."

"Not my sty," Tamworth's voice was gentle. "Welcome to Pig House, brother."

They retired together and closed the door, leaving a restless and inquiring crowd outside.

"Let's count the seconds," Hedgecock said to Thomas.

They counted up to a hundred eighteen times before the Minister and Tamworth emerged. The crowd rushed forward; Blossom and Thomas crept under Joe for shelter.

"What did you talk about? How did it go? Did you decide anything? What did you say? Have you come to an agreement?"

"We'll let you know later," the Minister smiled. "There will be a report. Right now there are tea and refreshments for everyone, being served at the farm."

There was a mad rush to the dairy where tea, biscuits, ice-cream and lemonade were being handed out by various assorted ladies and the dairy maids in their pink nylon overalls. Mrs. Baggs was charging high prices and hoping to make a good profit.

"What a lovely day," everyone said.

The lovely day was followed by one of those perfect evenings, blue and golden, that we get from time to time in England, just to remind us that it is a green and pleasant land. The Minister returned to London. The crowds went home and so did Blossom and Thomas. They played for a while and then decided to go back to Tamworth.

He was glad to see them.

"I feel restless. I can't settle down after all the excitement. I keep composing speeches and then I can't finish them. And Mrs. Baggs had a very nasty look in her eye when she brought in my food just now."

Blossom gave him some apples.

"Many thanks. I do like apples so much. But best of all, I think, I like a cabbage."

"We'll remember next time," Blossom promised.

"If you don't mind," Tamworth said, "I'd like to go for a walk. Will you come with me?"

"Yes, if I can ride on your back."

"Of course, my young friend. Leap on."

Leaping was hardly the word to describe getting on to Tamworth's back, but Thomas managed it quite well. He'd had plenty of practice.

They jogged over the fields and into the lane, Tamworth chuffing cheerily as they went along and Thomas waving hedge-parsley over them to keep off the flies.

At last Blossom said. "Just what did you and the Minister talk about, Tamworth?"

There was a roar of a powerful engine. Round the corner zoomed a motor-bike. Unable to stop, its rider crashed straight into Tamworth's huge and shapely form. The pig stood unshaken though he let out one terrible squeal. Thomas flew straight off into the ditch, full after the heavy rains, and landed squelching amid hedge-parsley, ground-ivy, foxgloves and willow-herb, to be joined by the motor-cyclist, and the pair sat glaring at each other in the ditch with garlands of up-rooted flowers round their heads while the motor-bike, far more damaged than Tamworth, lay uselessly on the grassy verge.

"Are you hurt, Tamworth?" Blossom cried. "Are you all right, Thomas?"

She ran from one to the other, waving her hands.

"I find myself undamaged," Tamworth said, after he had investigated all his trotters to see if they were still intact. "But I shall never forgive myself for that terrible squeal. It will ring in my ears till my dying day. I have never squealed in my life up till now, and I pray that I never shall again. But let us help Thomas and this unwary speedway rider out of the ditch."

However, they were already climbing out, unhurt but rather dazed, plucking flowers from their shirts, their trousers, and their shoes. The cyclist regarded the others all with horror.

"To hit a pig," he moaned. "All these years accident free and I have to hit a pig. With a boy riding it. I must be going crazy! I'm off for the police."

With difficulty he hauled up his bike and tried to start it, but no mere motor-bike could survive a head-on collision with Tamworth, so he put it down again, shook his fist at Tamworth and set off down the road.

"My good friend," Tamworth shouted, hurrying after him, "wait and see if we can help you."

It was no use, for they couldn't catch him.

"This will bring trouble," Thomas muttered, pulling a piece of willow-herb out of his mouth. "I know it will."

He was right. The motor-cyclist complained to the Sergeant at the Station, who immediately recognized Tamworth from the description. A claim was made to Farmer Baggs for the sum of one hundred pound's-worth of damage to the motor-bike caused by a menace to the public, namely a large pig with a small boy on its back.

"Pride had to come before a fall," Tamworth said. "I was too cocky after the Minister's visit."

The motor-cyclist did not get his hundred-pound claim awarded to him, but Mrs. Baggs said many nasty words and chalked up another bad mark against Tamworth.

Chapter Eleven

————————————— * —————————————

During the following week, Tamworth was asked to appear on television. On the morning that he was due to go on, Thomas found him greatly agitated.

"What's the matter?" he asked the pig, who was scratching furiously with his front trotter.

"I've got dandruff. Horrible, itchy dandruff, I'm covered in it. There I am, about to appear before an audience of millions, and I've got dandruff. Thomas, what shall I do?"

"That's easy enough. Mother uses a medicated shampoo on us. I'll go and get it."

He shot back home and returned with a bottle of shampoo and a scrubbing brush.

"Hang on," and he once more went home to return weighed down with two buckets of water. Before Tamworth could protest he poured a bucketful straight over him.

"Ouch, ow, ow," spluttered and spat the pig, for the sudden cascade was absolutely icy. Thomas had forgotten to use the hot tap. Unmoved, he then upended the entire bottle of shampoo and started to scrub. He rubbed and dubbed till lather bubbled and blew in all directions. Tamworth moaned piteously. No one

would have taken him for the President at that moment.

"It's going in my eyes."

"Mummy always tells us to be brave."

"It's difficult under such circumstances."

"Shan't be long. I've done you really well. Next your ears. They're important. Now for the rinsing."

Thomas flung the other bucket of cold water over the unhappy animal.

"Oh save me, someone. Help!"

No one heeded his cries and Thomas rubbed him remorselessly with one of the best bath towels. Mummy was rather annoyed about that when she found out later.

"Now sit in the sun and dry. You'll feel very nice soon. I got rid of nearly all the dandruff."

Thomas inspected the shivering pig. Even his ears hung down for once, but slowly the sun warmed him and his bristles dried. He shook himself. Yes, he did feel better.

"Oh, you look beautiful. You're the handsomest as well as the cleverest pig in the world."

"You really think so?"

Tamworth loved admiration. He did, indeed, look well. His red-gold coat shone in the sun, and his ears pricked up into furry points.

"What time is the programme?"

"Eight o'clock. I've got a good showing time. The van will soon be coming to fetch me. This is a great day. I, the President of the Animals' Union, shall address the Nation."

"We'll be watching," Thomas promised.

Throughout the land the sets were flickering merrily before the great British public. Thomas and Blossom sat in complete harmony on the same chair, together with Hedgecock and Mr. Rab. Mummy and Daddy were also watching and so were most of the neigh-

89

bours. But one household, at least, was not so pleased. Mrs. Baggs was furious that no one had asked her husband to take part in the programme. She had shaken her fist at the van that came to take Tamworth to the television studio. Christopher Robin and Lurcher had booed, but Joe, Barry McKenzie and Ethelberta chorused, "Good luck, Tamworth," as he drove away.

Mr. Baggs was not sorry at all that he had not been invited. He hated speeches and furthermore he was feeling ill that evening. He just wished his wife would stop grumbling, and that his head would stop aching. But the Baggs family, too, sat in their chairs like the rest, and watched.

At eight o'clock the Minister came on to open the programme.

"I have come here tonight to introduce my good friend, Tamworth Pig, who has some interesting schemes of his own to put forward. I do not agree with all of them, but some could bring extra prosperity to this country. However, let our eloquent friend speak for himself. Here, ladies and gentlemen, is Tamworth Pig."

Cameras panned to the handsome, porcine face with its smiling snout.

"Oh, he does look nice," Blossom whispered. "I wish we had colour television."

"I shampooed him while you were at school," Thomas hissed.

"You used my best bath towel."

Mummy was still bitter about this.

"Sh! Listen. He's about to start."

"I have come here, this evening, to ask for your help, to carry out the ideas I have in mind. Wherever we turn today we are faced with the fact that half the people of the world do not get enough to eat. Now, food is one of the best things in life. A good, tasty meal gives one a warm glow inside. Well-fed humans and animals may not be happy but at least they have a chance to be. Hungry humans and animals have no chance at all. They can only think food. They can't really think about any of the important things in life because they only feel hungry, hungry, hungry, and wonder where the next meal is coming from.

"Now in this country are many fine farmers and gardeners and food manufacturers who are doing a good job. Men like my good friend Farmer Baggs, who work hard."

" 'Ear! 'Ear!" Farmer Baggs said to his wife.

"Yet much more could be done. Let every man and woman, child and animal in the country try to produce more food, grub, as another friend of mine, Thomas, calls it."

Here Thomas went bright red and hid his face in the chair.

"Let us fill every space, every unused bit of country and waste ground in our towns, with food, oomptious, scrumptious food. I have composed a little song which goes to the tune of John Brown's body.

Let us grow more grub today, more and more and more,
Wheat and fruit and vegetables, potatoes by the score,

With bread and cakes and sweets galore, more than you
*   ever saw,*
                    Grow more grub today!
                    Grow more, grow more,
                    Hallelujah!

"If you would like further details of my scheme, including how we send extra food to other lands, I have written a leaflet, beautifully illustrated by another friend, Blossom."

Here it was Blossom's turn to blush.

"Including my invention of a new type of super-heated greenhouse, and a streamlined factory for producing an entirely new kind of sweet, invented by myself, which does NOT make teeth decay. I have called it Pig's Delight, and I hope that children, especially, will like it.

"Give your animals, give us, a chance to share in the benefits of extra food. Improve our food and we'll improve yours even more, with better eggs, milk, everything.

"And now I come to my final point. I am sure that meat is bad for you. I know you love your roast dinner but"—here Tamworth's voice trembled—"roast pork will kill you as it will surely kill me. Let us give you cheese, butter, milk, eggs, but not meat. And if you ask, as well you may, well, what does a pig give if not bacon, sausages and pork? Then I ask in reply, do you eat your dog, your cat, your budgerigar, your pony? Make us pigs pets like them. We shall not disappoint you. We are clean, intelligent companions.

Make us your pets, not your dinners! May you choose wisely. I shall abide by your choice."

"Hurrah for Tamworth!" Thomas shouted.

"It's all right for you, you don't like meat. I do," Blossom said.

"It won't make a happorth of difference anyway," Daddy said. "But it was a good speech, even though he'll never get very far with it. He needs to work out his ideas more fully."

"I think I could have written a better song than he did," Mr. Rab muttered jealously to himself.

In bed, Thomas hugged Num and said, "Don't sing the bedtime song yet. I want to hear the van bring Tamworth home."

"Thomas," Mr. Rab said. "You know my special worried feeling I get. . . ."

"Humph!" Hedgecock snorted. "Rubbish."

"Well, I've got it about Tamworth," went on Mr. Rab. "There's danger about somewhere."

Just then, they all heard the van drive safely past, and so they fell asleep.

Chapter Twelve

———————————*———————————

Blossom, Thomas, Hedgecock and Mr. Rab were playing Ludo in the shed. They had just reached the point where Thomas was shouting with rage because Blossom had thrown three sixes in a row when there came a clatter of hoofs and a loud banging on the door. Ludo forgotten, they rushed to open. There stood Barry McKenzie Goat.

"Come. Come quick. Mrs. Baggs has captured Tamworth and locked him in the concrete hut. You know, the one beside the barns. And she's sent for the slaughterers. She says she's going to . . . to . . ."

"To what?" they cried.

"Make him into bacon and she'll eat him. Every bit. Come on."

They started to run as fast as they could towards the farm.

"What does Mr. Baggs say? Surely he won't let them kill Tamworth," Blossom panted.

"He's got 'flu and he's in bed. He doesn't know anything about it."

They ran on, red and breathless, till they reached Pig House. Blossom could not bear to look at the damson tree. Suppose Tamworth never sat there again —but that was too awful to contemplate.

"How long have we got?"

"Mr. Peasepoint, the slaughterer, lives about ten miles away. He's a busy man and he may not be able to come at once," Barry McKenzie answered.

"Is anybody guarding Tamworth?" Thomas asked.

"Christopher Robin Baggs and Lurcher Dench are on the roof armed with pitchforks."

"Oh no. How awful."

Blossom shuddered and then took a deep breath.

"We must decide on the best course of action. Barry, you fetch Joe and Fanny Cow. Thomas, you see if you can creep in to see Mr. Baggs and tell him what's going on. I'll ring up the newspapers and television studios. Surely they won't let Tamworth be killed."

"I wouldn't count on that," Hedgecock grunted. "I'm going to get a clothes-line to tie up those two boys."

"Good idea. Where shall we meet again, Blossom?" Thomas asked.

"Behind the haystack, near the shed."

Blossom ran to the nearest telephone kiosk and dialled 999.

"Which service do you require, fire, police or ambulance?" a voice asked.

"All of them! Send the lot to Baggs's Farm, Rubble Lane, where a murder is about to be committed. Hurry, please, hurry."

She banged down the receiver and ran home calling "Mummy" as she entered the house, but it was empty. She seized the directory and looked up the numbers of all the newspapers she knew.

"This is going to take some time," she murmured to herself as she put on her determined look and started dialling. "I hope Mr. Peasepoint gets a puncture in his tyres."

Meanwhile Thomas had crept quietly up to the side door of the farmhouse, which he knew was seldom used. It led to the hall and stairs. Everywhere was silent. Christopher Robin was guarding Tamworth and Mrs. Baggs was probably in the kitchen. He stole slowly up the stairs. One creaked, and, outside, Rover started to bark. Thomas paused, his heart beating so loudly he was sure someone would hear it, but no one came and he reached the landing where eight identical brown doors, all shut, confronted him. He opened one cautiously and peeped into the bathroom. He had to try all the other seven before he found the room where Mr. Baggs lay on a brass-knobbed bedstead with his eyes closed and his red face streaked with perspiration. He groaned at intervals and Thomas shook his arm.

"Mr. Baggs. You've got to get up. We need you. You've got to save Tamworth. Please wake up."

But Mr. Baggs only moaned and muttered, "Mangle worzels with the taties. Mangle worzels with the taties."

Thomas shook him again.

"Mr. Baggs! Mr. Baggs! Please wake up."

Mr. Baggs shivered so much that the eiderdown fell off the bed.

"I'm the queen of the May, Mother," he sang with the sweat running off his forehead.

Thomas wiped his face with a cloth from the bedside chair and replaced the eiderdown. It was clear that Mr. Baggs was going to be no help at all. Then he heard Mrs. Baggs coming up the stairs. He shot under the bed, trying not to breathe as she stumped round

the room. He could see her fat ankles bulging over her black-laced shoes, so he shut his eyes and prayed for her to go away. When he opened them, the feet had disappeared. He tiptoed down the stairs and out of the house. Then he ran like the wind to where the little band of rescuers was waiting.

On the shed's flat roof Lurcher and Christopher Robin were enjoying themselves hugely. They had always been afraid of Tamworth before, because he could always get at them in his field, but now he was captured and they were taking their revenge. Through a small aperture, not nearly large enough to allow Tamworth to escape, they were poking pitchforks, jabbing viciously at where they thought the pig to be.

"Yah! Fatty! Fatty Pig! Old Ginger Snout! Bristly chops! Ginger Belly! We'll have you. Take that! And that!"

They thrust and pushed and jabbed.

Tamworth sat unmoving and with immense dignity in the farthest, darkest corner. He had stuck an old piece of corrugated iron as a shield in front of himself, and was reciting a long Latin poem.

"Fatty! Are you listening, Fatty? We'll have you fried for breakfast, Fatty. Thought you were a clever pig, didn't you? Well, you're just a stupid old fool pig, aren't you? You didn't think we'd catch you, did you, Fatty?"

Tamworth spoke quietly to himself. "There are other words they could use. I can think of great, large, immense, enormous, tremendous, vast, huge, Mammoth-like, Gargantuan, Herculean, well-built, portly, ample, abundant, bulky, massive, gigantic, magnificent, leviathan, giant, mighty, corpulent, stout, plump, brawny, whacking, whopping, colossus, hippopotamus, Brobdingnagian pig, to mention a few. Then one could round off with fine, big pig."

"Shut up, Fatty. Silly ole Fatty. Who didn't know Mrs. Baggs had got a net, eh? Silly old Fatty. Caught you in it nicely, didn't she, Fatty? Yah—yah—there—take—that—and—that!"

"It was not, I admit, one of my happiest moments

98

when I was caught in the net, but a philosopher such as myself remains calm in all circumstances, however unpleasant. At least I did not squeal. I could not have forgiven myself if I had squealed."

"You'll squeal soon enough when they pig-stick you," Lurcher yelled, dancing with delight on the roof.

Suddenly he found he was dancing in the air and descending rapidly to the ground, where Joe appeared from behind the shed just in time to place one hoof, quite gently, in the middle of his back. Thomas had butted him straight off the roof. At the same time Christopher Robin Baggs, too, found himself propelled off the roof by the hands of Blossom, fierce and fighting for once with all her weight behind her. The pitchforks, Blossom's main worry, flew harmlessly through the air. She and Thomas had climbed up on to the roof behind the two boys, who were so busy shouting they'd heard nothing.

Fanny Cow waited lovingly for Christopher Robin to stand upright so that she could give him a little nudge with her horns and knock him down again, where she stood over him, chewing her cud ruminatingly. He wept, but Lurcher was made of sterner stuff and he shouted loudly:

"Mrs. Baggs! Help! Come quick, Mrs. Baggs!"

"Tie them up with the clothes-line," Hedgecock commanded and they lashed the two boys together.

"I've brought some elastoplast in case Tamworth was hurt," Blossom said.

"Put it on their mouths," Mr. Rab squeaked, quite entering into the spirit of the operation.

They did as he suggested and the boys lay silent and helpless.

But Mrs. Baggs had heard the cry for help and was now running towards them. When she saw the boys, she shrieked:

"I'll have the law on you for this."

She doubled back to the house and dialled the police station.

"Send some men to Baggs's Farm, Rubble Lane, at once."

The policeman at the other end scratched his head.

"We've already sent one lot on its way out there. Ah, well, the more the merrier."

Mrs. Baggs rushed outside again, followed by two dairy maids. Barry McKenzie and Fanny moved forward, chased them into a corner and stood over them, horns lowered.

"Get Tamworth out of there, while we hold the women back," Barry called.

Blossom fumbled with the door.

"I can't open it. It's padlocked. What shall we do?"

Then there was a noble and fearful sight. Joe turned round, backed up to the door, looking over his shoulder to judge the distance and then kicked back with his mighty hooves. The door shook, came off its hinges and fell in splinters. Pieces of wood flew over Tamworth, who sat calmly behind his corrugated-iron shield reciting this line over and over again:

"To be, or not to be, that is the question."

"Ah, my good and faithful friends. I knew you would not desert me in my hour of need."

He shook bits of shattered wood off himself and emerged from his prison. Mrs. Baggs tried to wrap her apron over Barry's horns but he tossed it back over her head.

"I'll help too," squawked Ethelberta, flying up and scurrying round in circles. "I wish I'd known all about this earlier. I've always wanted to fly on to Mrs. Baggs's head. What fun. Wheeee. Cluck-cluck."

Then, suddenly, the air was filled with the hee-hawing blare of an ambulance, followed by two police cars and a fire-engine. The whole countryside re-echoed as brakes screeched and vehicles skidded to a halt wherever they could in the farmyard. Once again Mrs. Baggs's herbaceous borders were flattened. Several uniformed men jumped out and advanced upon the scene.

"Is this Baggs's Farm?" the first policeman asked.

"Yes," everyone shouted, including Mrs. Baggs, who had managed to get the apron off her head.

"What's all the trouble, then?" he said, taking out his notebook.

Everyone rushed forward and started to speak at once, except Christopher Robin and Lurcher who were tied together on the ground, but, at that moment, the loud hee-hawing of a police car again rent the air as another contingent of constables drove into the farmyard and dismounted.

"Is this Baggs's Farm?" one of them asked.

"Yes," everyone shouted.

"What's the trouble, then?" he asked, taking out his notebook, and he advanced towards the first policeman until they almost stood face to face.

Two ambulance men emerged with a stretcher, looked round for a casualty, saw the two tied-up bodies, put them on the stretcher and disappeared with them into the ambulance.

Several firemen in search of a fire had erected ladders against the side of the house and were ascending them.

Two vans now drove up, just managing to get into the farmyard. One had "Wessex Television" on the side while the other bore the legend "Daily Moan". More men jumped out and joined the ever-increasing throng.

"Where's the TV Pig?" one man shouted.

Television cameras whirred, only to be drowned by the drone of a helicopter overhead. The BBC had arrived in style, but, unfortunately, there was no room left in the farmyard for a helicopter and they had to land in a nearby field.

The police were trying to establish some kind of order. They had persuaded Barry and Fanny Cow to allow Mrs. Baggs and her dairy maids out of their corner and now a circle formed round the silent form of Tamworth.

Blossom had seized P.C. Cubbins, a friend and ally for most of her life, and was shaking his sleeve furiously.

"She's going to kill Tamworth. You've got to stop her."

"It's my farm and my pig. Get these trespassers out of 'ere. All of 'em," Mrs. Baggs shouted, digging P.C. Spriggs with her elbow.

"She can't slaughter him, can she?" Blossom im-implored, her brown eyes wide.

"I don't know, Blossom, dear," P.C. Cubbins replied. "You see, I must do my duty."

He and P.C. Spriggs glared at one another, their chests almost meeting. It was clear which side each one favoured.

"Mrs. Baggs is entitled to do what she likes with her own property, namely one pig," Spriggs said emphatically.

Thomas glared at him, for they were old enemies.

"She's a wicked, mean woman. And Tamworth doesn't belong to her, he belongs to Farmer Baggs. You've got to see him first."

"You've got a lot to say, young Thomas," P.C. Spriggs declared. "I should think a lot of people are interfering in the Baggs's own business. And I should very much like to know who brought all this crowd here."

He stared hard and long at Blossom, who went bright red and hid her face against P.C. Cubbins's sleeve.

"Let me 'ave that pig!" Mrs. Baggs shouted.

The pig in question had a strange look on his face. He seemed to have entered into a dream, to be looking out far beyond all the farmyard turmoil.

Yet one more van squeezed into the lane and out stepped a very well-dressed gentleman with a kindly, smiling face. He pushed through the throng and came up to the main group.

"I'm Mr. Peasepoint," he beamed. "You must be Mrs. Baggs. Delighted, delighted to meet you. Dear me, what a lot of people here. I'm afraid I shall have to ask them to leave before I can carry out my good work."

Tamworth stood erect, his face altered and strange. The crowd moved back, as he spoke.

"It seems I am to die. So be it. I die for a Cause, and so I shall die proudly. I shall not squeal. Dear friends, I bid you farewell, Joe and Fanny and Barry. Don't cry, Mr. Rab. Good-bye, Hedgecock. God bless you, dearest Blossom and my esteemed friend and ally Thomas. Remember the cause, boy, remember the cause."

There was a long silence. Tears rained down Blossom's cheeks, but Thomas's eyes were blazing blue, his cheeks scarlet. He leapt, a wonderful jump, right on to Tamworth's back, where he stood shaking with fury.

"No! No! No! No! No! I won't let them kill you, Tamworth. You shan't die!"

He called up to the house, hands cupped round his mouth:

"Mr. Baggs! Mr. Baggs! Oh, do wake up, you stupid man!"

At the window above, conveniently opened by the firemen, who were still looking for the blaze, appeared the bleary visage of Farmer Baggs. He saw the crowd below, and a bewildered look spread over his face.

"Whatever's goin' on 'ere?" he said.

"That horrible, mean wife of yours is going to kill Tamworth," Thomas shouted.

Mr. Baggs paused, saw Mr. Peasepoint and he seemed to understand. The watchers below waited expectantly.

"Oh no 'er ain't. 'Er's been a-bullying of me and Tamworth for years, but 'er ain't a killing of nobody, neither me nor 'im. And now will you all go and git off my land. There ain't no peace anywhere and I want to git back to bed for me 'ead's fair a-killing of me. Maud, woman, come up yere and git me a nice, cool drop of

105

cider. That's what 'e should be a-doing, instead of filling me farm up with foolish people with nuthin' better to do."

The window slammed shut.

Thomas collapsed on Tamworth's back and wound his arms round the stout neck. The crowd made a path for them as they turned towards Pig House with Blossom and the others following behind.

An ancient man rode up on a matching bicycle. He was the reporter from the local paper, and even as he rode in the crowd was dispersing.

"Am I late again?" he asked.

"Yes," an irritable fireman replied as he coiled up his unused hose.

"I never do get to a happening, when it's happening," the old man sighed as he remounted his machine and pedalled slowly away.

Chapter Thirteen

———————————— * ————————————

It was the last day of the summer holidays and the children had taken along sandwiches, crisps, peanuts, lemonade and chocolate to have a picnic with Tamworth. They'd prepared a special bag for him containing an assortment of apples, cabbages, carrots and turnips. Blossom danced along, eyes a-sparkle, but Thomas trailed behind moodily, kicking stones as he went.

"Cheer up. It's a lovely day and we're having a picnic with Tamworth," Blossom said.

"Don't care. Shan't cheer up. Ugh! Cheer up she says. As if anyone could cheer up with school to-morrow."

Tamworth came trotting out of Pig House to greet them.

"Hello, my friends. Why, what's the matter, Thomas?"

"I'm fed up. It's horrible old school. I don't want to go to school. I just want everything to go on like it is now, for ever and ever."

Tamworth rooted in the bag and selected the best cabbage. When he had finished it he sat down under the damson tree and looked at Thomas, who was eating nothing. Blossom had already eaten four sandwiches and a bag of crisps.

"Oh, Thomas," he said. "Everything changes. It has to. It's the way of things. It won't be so bad at school, in fact, you'll enjoy it once you're there again."

"The only things I shall enjoy are bashing old Baggsy and pulling Gwendolyn horrible Twitchie's hair."

"You mean horrible hair," Hedgecock put in.

"No I don't. I mean Gwendolyn, horrible, Twitchie," Thomas snapped.

"Well, I know something you'll like," Tamworth said.

He went into Pig House and emerged with a football, dribbling it mostly between his trotters.

"Where did you get that?" Blossom asked, her mouth full of chocolate.

She'd almost finished her share of the picnic.

"It was sent to me by one of my many admirers. Come on, everyone. We're going to play football and give Thomas lots of practice."

Thomas still looked sulky, so Tamworth flipped the ball at him with his snout. He looked so funny that a grin began to spread over Thomas's face, and he too, ran forward, took a mighty kick and sent the ball high over Pig House. In no time at all, two sweaters were down as goal posts and everyone was running and kicking like mad.

At last Tamworth stopped, puffing like a steam-engine.

"I'm losing pounds of beautiful fat. I shall have to

have some more sustenance," he panted, as he searched in the bag for another cabbage.

Everyone collapsed, red, sweaty and cheerful, and finished the rest of the picnic.

"And now I've got another surprise for you. Come into Pig House," Tamworth said.

They went inside, and there on a box stood a transistor radio. Tamworth turned the knob and music blared forth.

"It's a beauty. Where did you get it?" Mr. Rab asked.

"The Vegetarian Society presented it to me for my work in trying to stop people eating meat."

He looked very pleased with himself.

"I want you to listen to the news, which is on in a minute. Sit down all of you."

They sat down and listened quietly. At last the music stopped and the newsreader came on. He read out several items of news and Mr. Rab began to fidget because he found it boring, but Hedgecock nudged him sharply. Then came the item Tamworth was waiting for and he turned up the volume.

"After a debate in Parliament yesterday, it was decided to start a campaign for 'Grow more food' in Britain. A committee has been set up to promote food expansion and it will be advised by Tamworth Pig of Baggs's Farm."

"There," Tamworth said, and switched off the radio.

"Why, Tamworth, you've gone pink under your bristles!" Blossom said.

"Yes, I'm very pleased that my small efforts have not gone unnoticed. And I owe so much of this to you, dear friends."

He took the lid off a cardboard box and emptied out several parcels, all wrapped in blue and red paper decorated with white dancing pigs.

"So I have presents for you all. The Vicar's wife was kind enough to purchase them for me."

Blossom opened hers first and there inside was the prettiest, floppiest doll ever, with hair so soft you wanted to rub your face in it. She wore a little white gown with a blue ribbon round it to match her eyes.

"Oh, oh," was all Blossom could say.

She felt as if she could cry, it was so beautiful.

For Thomas there was a gloriously complicated train set with lots of points, gradients, stations, signals, engines and rolling stock. Mr. Rab had a book containing hundreds and hundreds of poems and for Hedgecock there was a compendium of games, including chess, draughts, ludo, snakes and ladders, tiddlywinks and dominoes.

They could hardly speak, it was such a surprise. Tamworth trotted back and forth poking his snout into everything, enjoying the presents just as much as they did, and he simultaneously played games with Hedgecock, dolls with Blossom, trains with Thomas and listened to Mr. Rab reading from his book.

Then he routed around in the box and pulled out one last parcel.

"The Vicar's wife also sent something else for you, Thomas. She says she hopes you'll be friends again."

With a huge grin, he handed over a box of chocolates.

Tamworth Pig Saves the Trees

Chapter One

———————— * ————————

It was Saturday and Thomas arose singing.

"No school. No school," he carolled through the house.

He pushed open the door of Daddy's and Mummy's bedroom.

"It's Saturday, Dad. You can lie in bed for a bit."

Dad opened a weary eye and reached out for the alarm clock at the side of the bed. He shook it incredulously.

"Why, it's only five to six."

"Yes, I know. I only came in to tell you, you didn't have to wake up early today, as it's Saturday."

Daddy groaned pitifully and pulled the bedclothes over his head.

"Go away, you horrible child," came a muffled cry.

Thomas trotted away, leaving the door open, not hearing the call behind him.

"And close the door!"

He was too busy shaking his head and muttering about the ingratitude of grown-ups, who never appreciated anything that one did for them. Still, Blossom should be ready to play by now.

Blossom, his sister, was a wonderful teller of tales

and inventor of games. Yesterday she had begun the story of Stringo, the little boy made of string, and Thomas wanted to hear more of it. He opened her door. Gentle snuffles whiffled through the quiet room. He took a running leap and landed with his knees on her soft form. It was always pleasant jumping on Blossom. She was so plump and comfortable, just like a pillow, he thought. He felt quite fond of her, but, strangely enough, she didn't seem fond of him. Flushed with sleep, brown eyes full of tears, she pushed and kicked him off the bed.

"I was having a wonderful dream and now you've spoilt it. Go away, you horrible boy!"

Hurt, he stared at her, then walked out of the room. He didn't like being told to go away twice like that. People were peculiar, he decided as he made his way down to the kitchen.

Breakfast was obviously hours away, so he helped himself to his favourite cereal, pouring nearly all the packet into the largest Pyrex bowl, the one his mother made apple pies in. Some cereal fell on the floor where it made an extremely pleasing, scrunchy noise under his feet.

"Scrunchy, munchy, chunchy, grunchy," he murmured contentedly.

The sugar bowl was almost empty, so he found the sugar bag and tore it open. This proved difficult at first, so he pulled extra hard and the bag split right down the side, spilling half on the table. He scooped this on to the floor and turned to get the milk. There was only a pint left and he must leave some for Mummy's early cup of tea. A bargain offer of an inflatable boat on the cereal packet caught his eye and he proceeded to read it as he poured out the milk. When he looked down he was surprised to find he had used the whole pint. He tried to get some back into the bottle but it proved impossible, so he gave up, and started on his cereal, and soon the kitchen was filled with the noise of Thomas eating.

What next? A day of infinite possibilities lay ahead. He could climb a mountain, tame a lion, walk a tight-rope, score a goal for England. Contemplating all these, he went upstairs and flung his friends, the snoring Hedgecock and sniffling Mr. Rab, out of his bed. Hedgecock, as cantankerous and irritable as ever, snarled at him, while Mr. Rab, a long, thin rabbit wearing a red and white striped waistcoat and green bow tie, whimpered as he tried to climb back into warmth and comfort.

He whimpered even more when Thomas set up an indoor football game of his own invention, involving a very hard, tiny, rubber ball. He hated football. His skinny legs always got hurt. Poetry was the thing Mr. Rab loved best of all, and next to poetry, Thomas's sister Blossom and then Thomas. He didn't love Hedgecock at all.

Once aroused, Hedgecock played quite well, though sometimes the ball got lost among his feathery prickles. No one ever knew what Hedgecock really was, and as he became incredibly cross if anyone tried to find out, it remained a mystery. It was also difficult to discover what he actually liked as he grumbled so much about everything whatsoever, but he did enjoy counting and numbers, and utterly despised Mr. Rab and his poetry.

At half-time, Thomas decided the hanging bed-clothes were in the way, so he hauled them all off, dumped them in the bathroom next door, and continued with the game. Finally Thomas's team won six two. Hedgecock and Mr. Rab always let him win because if he lost he grew very angry and threw things and stamped and shouted. The game over, to Thomas's satisfaction and no loss of temper, he went to the window and looked out between the curtains.

The morning was thick and white like cotton wool. They could not even see the bottom of the garden. In a moment Thomas had hauled jeans and sweater over his pyjamas and pulled on the slippers he never wore in

the house. Urging Hedgecock and Mr. Rab before him, he hurried out into the mist, which thinned around them as they walked across the white lawn, leaving a green trail behind them. Spiders' webs clung wetly to their hands and faces.

"Season of mists and mellow fruitfulness," Mr. Rab cried suddenly in his special, high, poetry-reciting voice.

He stopped equally suddenly as Hedgecock kicked him.

"Can't we go anywhere without you reciting your rotten old poetry?"

"It's not fair. It's not fair. I love poetry. It's much better than your horrid counting. Why, you'd even count your own snores if you could."

"I don't snore," Hedgecock objected indignantly.

"Yes you do. You snore like . . . like ten thousand chain saws cutting down trees."

"I—do—not—snore."

"Oh, yes, you do."

Hedgecock kicked Mr. Rab much harder this time, so that he squealed.

"Shut up, you two," Thomas commanded. "We're going to see Tamworth Pig. I hope he's up and not asleep like everyone else."

Tamworth's favourite damson tree and Pig House, Tamworth's home, loomed unexpectedly out of the mist and there in the doorway stood the great pig himself, huge and golden, like some lesser sun. President of the Animals' Union, great campaigner for such causes as "Grow More Food and Eat Less Meat" (especially pork), he was the most famous pig in Britain and Thomas's friend and ally.

"Come in and have some Pig's Delight," he invited.

They went in and settled on the hay-strewn floor. Tamworth's home, which he refused to call a sty, was very comfortable and decorated with posters and photographs. A transistor radio stood on a handsome chest, both presents from the Vegetarian Society in gratitude for Tamworth's efforts to stop people eating meat. He had not succeeded yet, but he persevered. He

handed round a bag of Pig's Delight, a special sweet he had concocted for children which did not rot the teeth. It tasted delicious, rather like a mixture of chocolate, treacle, strawberries, mint, toffee and marshmallow.

"Thanks," Thomas muttered as he chewed. "I've brought you a cabbage. I picked it in the garden on the way here."

"Thank you, dear boy. You know how I appreciate a fine cabbage. And it's most welcome, for Mrs. Baggs, that extremely mean woman, who is supposed to feed

me, has not yet appeared with one of her inferior repasts."

"Now that you're famous and quite rich, I wonder you don't get someone kind to look after you. I wouldn't have her. Not after she tried to have you slaughtered."

"Oh, that doesn't worry me. She won't do that again and, after all, I do belong to Farmer Baggs. He's all right, a good, honest man, and I wouldn't want to upset him by changing things. What's more, I like it here."

Cabbage consumed, Tamworth sat back on his vast haunches. His eyes glittered and he wore a look of intense excitement. Thomas peered at him curiously.

"What's up?" he asked.

The giant pig tapped the floor with his neat little trotters. They all waited. At last he spoke in a deep voice.

"Last night I dreamed a dream. . . ."

"Like Joseph, you mean," put in Mr. Rab helpfully.

"Don't interrupt, you pink-nosed fool," Hedgecock snapped.

"In my dream, I saw the country below me."

"You were the ruler?"

It was Hedgecock interrupting this time. Mr. Rab pulled a face at him.

"Oh, no. I do not seek power. It would not be right for a pig to rule our country, though I should probably do no worse than some have done. No, the land was actually below me because I was flying over it in a kind of hovercraft."

"It must have been very strong to stand your weight."

Too late Mr. Rab put a hand over his mouth as though to push back his words, but Tamworth took no notice anyway. He was staring into the distance as though re-living his dream.

"And—and—dearest friends, there were no trees!" His voice shook with emotion.

"No trees? What do you mean?" Thomas asked.

"There were no trees to be seen. They'd all disappeared, been cut down, torn up, burnt, destroyed.

There were no forests, no woods, no commons, no shady gardens, no tree-lined parks. All, all were gone, the oak and the elm, the ash and the holly. There was no shade from the sun, no shelter from the storm, no branches for birds to nest in, nor for children to climb. There were no apples in Autumn, no trees for Christmas."

He paused, tears in his eyes.

"Don't be upset. It was only a dream. I have nasty ones sometimes. Forget it," Thomas said.

"I can't forget it. It was a vision of the future. Every day trees are destroyed. Every day trees are dying. We must save the trees," Tamworth cried.

A loud neighing was heard as the head of Joe the Shire Horse pushed through the aperture cut specially for him.

"What be 'ee goin' on about now, Tamworth?" he asked in his slow voice. "I 'eard 'ee talkin' on and on. I come to tell 'ee that Mrs. Baggs is just a-settin' out with your grub."

"Then I'm off," Thomas said, for Mrs. Baggs was no friend of his.

He stroked Tamworth's upstanding, furry ears.

"Cheer up. You don't want to worry about rotten old dreams."

"Don't you understand? I must start a new campaign. 'Grow more Food' is going well now. I can take time off for this newer, greater cause. Save the trees! Save the trees!" Tamworth cried, going to the door and gazing into the mist.

"I can only see the damson tree in this lot, and I

124

haven't heard of anyone threatening to cut that down,"
Hedgecock muttered.

The clank of a pail was heard. Mrs. Baggs was
approaching, so Thomas, Hedgecock and Mr. Rab
vanished rapidly into the fog.

"Tamworth's off again," Thomas said to Blossom as
he re-entered the kitchen.

She sat, scrubbed, pink and shining, behind a mound
of toast. Blossom dearly loved food.

"And so is Mum. You want to look out," she replied, licking the melting butter off her fingers.

"Why, what have I done?"

"I think she said that you'd made more mess before
breakfast than most children do in a day."

"Well, that's unfair. All I did was to come downstairs, bothering no one, get myself some grub and go
out. What's wrong with that?"

"That's not what she said you did. And if I were you, I'd change those slippers before she sees them."

"You're not me, and I don't want you to be, you great, fat, stupid girl. I don't care about slippers. I want to tell you about Tamworth."

"What about him?"

"He's got a new cause. He wants to save the trees."

"Is that you, Thomas?"

Mummy's voice was calling and her feet approaching. Thomas dived under the table, but it was no use. He was soon discovered. So, too, were his slippers.

Chapter Two

———————————————✳———————————————

Blossom sat back with a sigh of satisfaction, having just completed a banner, a huge creation mounted on two broom handles painted gold. The design was simple, a white background with "SAVE THE TREES" emblazoned on it in green. She laid it carefully on the floor to dry, together with two small pennants which read, "Planta Seeda Day" and "Keep Britain Green".

"There!" she said.

"They're jolly nice. I wish I could have written a poem on one," Mr. Rab said enviously.

"No one would be able to read it being marched along on a banner. You'd do better to write a marching song."

Mollified, Mr. Rab began to sing:

> *"I think that I shall never see*
> *A poem lovely as a tree."*

"Somebody's already written that one," Hedgecock growled.

"Come and help me clear up all this mess," Blossom said, eyeing the paints, rags, brushes and jars.

She was alone. Everyone had deserted her. Sighing, she pushed all the painting paraphernalia into the nearest cupboard, and wandered into the garden, where the sun beamed down on the dahlias, the chrysanthemums and the last roses. Saint Luke's little summer had arrived, in October, with some of the sunniest days of the year, before the equinoctial gales arrived to blow away the soft warmth and the mists, making way for winter.

"Let's go out, Mummy," she said, poking her head round the kitchen door where Mummy was surrounded by a quantity of flour, eggs, butter and bowls. Thomas was helping himself to some strips of raw pastry.

"Leave it alone, Thomas. There'll be none left. No, Blossom, I can't go out just now. I must get a few things ready for those new people, the Postlewaithes. I've asked them to supper tonight so that they can meet some of our friends."

"I bet we'll only have toast for tea while you've got all this gorgeous grub. It's not fair. You're not much of a Mum, are you?"

"And you're not much of a son, are you? But we have to put up with you," Daddy said, coming in in his black, yellow, orange, green, pink and blue, accidentally-handpainted shirt. He had been decorating upstairs. He propelled Thomas through the door with a painted hand.

"A walk will do you good," he smiled firmly.

"Ugh," Thomas replied.

"Oh, come on, I'll race you to Pig House," Blossom cried.

Tamworth was indulging in an afternoon nap when they arrived panting. He opened half an eye, then closed it again.

"I've finished the 'Save the Trees' banners," Blossom whispered in his ear.

It flopped up and down, then Tamworth raised his enormous bulk.

"Thank you, indeed, Blossom. I've no doubt they're painted in your usual beautiful style. I've still got some of the posters you did for 'Grow More Food'."

"There were thirty-eight sausages on sticks," Hedgecock announced suddenly for no apparent reason.

"Shush!" Thomas, Blossom and Mr. Rab exclaimed simultaneously, looking nervously at Tamworth, who hated any mention of sausages, pork or bacon or any of his future possibilities. Fortunately, he did not appear to have heard.

"Let's go conkering," Thomas suggested.

"Conquering what?" Hedgecock asked.

"Getting conkers, he means, stupid. You know, those brown nuts that grow on trees," Mr. Rab said.

He yelped as Hedgecock bashed him.

"Come on, then. Where shall we go?" Blossom asked, stroking Mr. Rab soothingly.

"The Tumbling Wood is the best place, I think. There are some very fine trees there. Wait, I'll get a basket," Tamworth said.

They ran, jumped and skipped over the stream where Thomas had once nearly drowned an entire mole colony, through the Rainbow Field, so named because of its curved shape, and over Hunter's Bridge on to the rough track that led to the Tumbling Wood, which covered the highest hill in the neighbourhood and so gave the wood its name, for the trees looked as if they were tumbling down the hillside.

"Look at those beautiful trees," Tamworth said.

They all looked, even Hedgecock. Leaves were brown and yellow and gold against the blue sky. Trunks shone silver.

"Oh, come on," grunted the bored Hedgecock.

There were too many trees for him to count and any other beauty meant nothing at all to him. They ran into the wood.

"There's hundreds of conkers," Thomas cried and, for a while, there was silence as they looked and scrambled under the leaves for the glossy, brown nuts.

Hedgecock counted furiously; Mr. Rab held up a particularly magnificent specimen.

"Isn't it a beauty? I bet a fairy polished this one."

Hedgecock nearly choked.

"Fairy poppycock. Huh! You know fairies aren't real. Not like us."

Thomas put the extra large conker in his pocket instead of the basket.

"It is a good one, though. I'll ask Mum to bake this one for me, then I can use it in the conker fights at school."

"We've got ninety-eight altogether," Hedgecock said.

"Two more, then, and that's enough," Tamworth ruled.

"I'm going to hit that one on that branch," Thomas shouted.

He threw up a short stick and missed. He flung the stick again with extra force and half the branch broke off, descending on the head of Mr. Rab, dancing below. He fell in a heap, thin little paws twitching feebly in the twigs and leaves.

"Oh, poor Mr. Rab," Blossom cried, flinging aside the branch.

There was a piteous groan.

"He's all right. Get up, stripy," Hedgecock snorted.

"His poor nose has gone white," Blossom exclaimed, investigating the frail form for breaks or sprains.

He sank back in her arms, relishing all the attention that was being showered upon him.

"Looks like a blooming corpse," Hedgecock agreed, peering closely. "No, he's coming round. His nose is going that nasty, pink, blancmange colour again."

Tamworth, too, inspected Mr. Rab and pronounced

him free from fatal injury, and Hedgecock pushed him into a sitting position with his snout. Finally he was ready to carry on.

Blossom found a good collection of old sweets in her pockets, for she always believed in keeping some in reserve in case of emergencies, and they wandered slowly out of the wood, eating blackberries and boiled sweets together, an interesting mixture.

Mr. Rab groaned carefully from time to time as they went along, just in case anyone should forget that he had been severely injured. Hedgecock was pretending to suck from an acorn pipe. The path turned sharply. Before them stood a huge machine—a bulldozer!

Tamworth stopped short.

"I wonder what this machine is doing here? Surely they don't intend to use it in this wood. Why, it has stood here since the days of the Romans and earlier still. Thomas, my boy, I don't like the look of that bulldozer."

"Let's wreck it," Thomas suggested hopefully.

"Certainly not. No vandalism. Come, it's time to return home. I think I must prepare a speech this evening."

They walked on slowly, then Hedgecock suddenly stopped.

"What's that stupid animal doing now? What a nuisance he is!"

They all looked round but there was no sign of Mr. Rab, so they retraced their steps to where they last remembered seeing him.

"Come on, Mr. Rab. It's time to go," Thomas called.

There was no reply.

"Do you think he's all right?" Blossom asked anxiously.

"It's fatal to take him to the woods," Hedgecock sighed. "He always wants to join the real rabbits. I bet that's what he's done now. And if he finds any, they'll only make fun of him. They always do."

"Come on, Mr. Rab," Thomas called again.

Hedgecock grumbled on.

"He's got no sense at all. He never did have. I don't go gallivanting with hedgehogs. I only met one once, and I couldn't stand the fellow. He couldn't count at all. Didn't even know how many paws he'd got."

The others were busy searching behind every bush and tree as he went on talking.

"Let's all shout together," Blossom suggested.

"One—two—three—go!"

"MR. RAB!"

The words re-echoed round the woods.

A thin form hurried from behind an elderberry bush. It was Mr. Rab, looking both pleased and sheepish, injuries forgotten.

"So sorry. So sorry. So sorry," he squeaked.

"Stop apologizing and come on. Where did you get to?" Thomas said.

"I've found a friend. A friend! He liked me. He really did. I'm going to see him again. He's got the sweetest little burrow."

"What sort of friend is he? Not a weasel or someone like that?"

Tamworth's voice was anxious, for he had no faith in Mr. Rab's ability to choose the right sort of friend. Neither had anyone else.

"Oh, no. He's really a nice rabbit, but he has a funny way of talking because he's a Welsh rabbit."

"Lumme," Hedgecock exclaimed. "That's all we needed, Mr. Rab and a Welsh rabbit. I hope he doesn't turn into a fox's dinner."

"Don't be unkind. There's no reason why Mr. Rab shouldn't have a friend."

"I agree with you, Tamworth. We'll take you to see him again, Mr. Rab." Blossom smiled at the excited creature.

"Not if I can help it," Hedgecock snorted.

Tamworth looked at the setting sun.

"I think we'd better hurry," he said.

An early bedtime had been indicated for Thomas because he had a knack of wrecking social occasions and Mummy did not want her evening ruined. Blossom was to be allowed to stay up for a while, so Thomas was in a wicked mood.

"It's not fair," he muttered as he settled into bed with Hedgecock and Mr. Rab.

"She's older than you," Mr. Rab pointed out.

"Yes, but much stupider."

He wrapped himself in Num, his soft square of grey blanket that stayed under the pillow and only came out at night. Very few friends were allowed to see Num.

Downstairs the Postlewaithes had arrived, eager to be friendly. They had no children of their own.

"I'd love to meet your little boy, too," Mrs. Postlewaithe cooed after she had been introduced to Blossom. "Can't I just peep at him in bed?"

"No," Daddy said.

"Oh, I know you don't really mean that. I'll just creep up on my own."

"I shouldn't bother," Daddy said, but he was weakening. Mrs. Postlewaithe was very pretty.

"I'll find the door," she said with a smile and tripped away.

Daddy put down his glass and followed. She found the right door, the one with all the finger marks on it, and peeped in. A small boy with very untidy hair, covered in an old, grey blanket, glared back at her. Six or seven spikes protruded from his mouth.

"Oh dear! Oh, you poor child. I didn't know you were afflicted. Whatever's wrong?"

She ran towards the bed.

Thomas, who hated anyone to see Num, snatched at it furiously to stuff it under the pillow, snarling through the sausages on sticks in his mouth. A wide

assortment of peanuts, olives, cheese biscuits and rolls, all in very crumbled condition, fell on the floor as Daddy arrived through the door.

Downstairs, Mummy exclaimed to the dutifully helpful Blossom:

"Why, half the food's disappeared!"

Much later, Hedgecock looked out cautiously from his blanket of knitted squares.

"It's all right now. They're making a lot of noise downstairs. It's a good job that female person was there or it would have been much worse."

"Yes," Thomas agreed. "Sing the bedtime song, Mr. Rab. I need it after Daddy's thrown all my food in the bin. It's not fair. All that food for them but nothing for me."

Mr. Rab sang the song he had made up long ago when Thomas was little.

"Mr. Rab has gone to sleep
Tucked in his tiny bed,
He has curled up his little paws
And laid down his sleepy head."

"Ugh, what muck," Hedgecock growled.

Sometimes, these days, Thomas thought himself much too old for Mr. Rab's song, but when things went wrong, he still liked to hear it. It felt comforting, like Num.

But back at school, things went well, for the huge conker, soaked in vinegar, baked hard and polished, defeated all challengers and became Super Conk, the champion.

"I think it was because the fairies polished it specially," Mr. Rab said.

"Fairy poppycock," Hedgecock snapped.

"No, fairy thistledown," Mr. Rab sniggered.

He did not often make a little joke and he soon regretted it as Hedgecock kicked him sharply.

Chapter Three

*

Blossom's banner was bright in the sunlight and the pennants fluttered in the gentle breeze. St. Luke's little summer had continued its fine efforts for several more days, which was a good omen for Tamworth Pig's march, now winding its way through the main street. It was to make a tour of the village to arrive at the ancient elm outside the 'Duck and Drake' where Tamworth was to make his speech.

The huge pig, bristles electric with excitement, led the way, followed closely by Blossom and Thomas carrying the two pennants, accompanied by Hedgecock and Mr. Rab. Next came the large banner borne aloft by Mrs. Postlewaithe and the Vicar's wife, who both believed in the importance of saving trees. They were followed by sixteen students from the local technical college and two archaeological students taking time off from a nearby dig. Nearly all Blossom's class had turned up to support the cause, but only one from Thomas's, a professor's son who had brought his father along. Both were very short-sighted, and thought the march was in aid of impoverished deep-sea fishermen.

138

Many animals came from the surrounding countryside, including one on a visit from Cornwall. Joe the Shire Horse, Barry McKenzie Goat and Fanny Cow brought up the rear of the procession to lend backs should anyone require aid and assistance along the way. Ethelberta Everready, the many-egg-laying hen, fluttered up and down the marching column, squawking happily. She loved any sort of goings on.

Thomas was tense and on the alert. All week he had endured taunts and jeers from Lurcher Dench and Christopher Robin Baggs, his old enemies, and had listened to threats of what they would do to the march. They would wreck it, they said. They would cause a riot. Eyes swivelling grimly from left to right, Thomas kept a look-out for all possible places of ambush.

P.C. Cubbins was also on the alert, walking along beside the procession. Fond as he was of Thomas and even fonder of dear Blossom, he was not at all sure that he approved of the whole business. The Vicar's wife was there, which lent it a respectable air but, still, you never knew. Many riots had been caused by people with the best of intentions.

On the other side of the column, P.C. Spriggs also marched along. His thoughts were quite straightforward. Any affair at all that had Thomas mixed up in it would run into trouble sooner or later. All he had to do was to await that moment.

But the march was moving peacefully along to the strains of a marching song composed by Mr. Rab.

"Save the trees!
Save the trees!
We're marching over here to save the trees.
Hand in hand and paw in paw,
Whether you've got two feet or four,
Raise your voice in a mighty roar
And save the trees!
Save the trees!"

The Vicar's wife's soprano soared magnificently above the rest as they turned the corner towards the elm tree where a small crowd awaited them. Thomas's eye ran over it warily, but it contained no enemies. He felt almost disappointed. He wouldn't have minded a scrap.

Tamworth mounted the small platform erected for him. Blossom watched anxiously, for she always worried about Tamworth's weight, but it seemed safe enough.

Tamworth's powerful voice rang out to the waiting crowd.

"Friends! Brothers! I come here today on behalf of other friends of ours. Beautiful, noble friends. Trees! And day by day, I regret to say, these beautiful, noble friends are being laid low."

He paused. Among the listening throng, there came a rustling and a ripple of movement eddying towards Tamworth as the crowd parted reluctantly to let some-one pass to the foot of the platform. A small, plump, extremely pretty, pink and black pig seated herself directly below Tamworth and gazed at him adoringly with her soft, dark eyes. She was panting a little.

Tamworth looked down at her, swallowed, then continued with his speech.

"Brothers! Friends! We are gathered here to talk about. . . ."

His voice faltered and stopped. He gazed at the pretty pig.

"What's your name?" he asked hoarsely.

"Melanie," she answered, lowering her long eyelashes.

"Melanie," Tamworth repeated as though in a dream.

The crowd was starting to grow restless.

"Get on with the speech," Thomas hissed at Tamworth, who gulped, looked at the crowd and began again.

"Friends! Brothers! We are here. . . ."

"We've heard all that. Tell us something new," a heckler shouted.

Blossom knew all Tamworth's speech, as he had rehearsed it with her.

"Plant a seed a day, whenever you can," she whispered to him.

"Plant a seed," Tamworth echoed vaguely, staring like a lost pig at Melanie.

"O! Lumme! He's gone nuts," Hedgecock said to Thomas.

"Yes. We'll have to do something quick."

As though in answer to a prayer, and it must have been the first time that this was ever the answer to anyone's prayer, came the roar of motor bikes. The local "Hell's Angels", leather-jacketed, black-helmeted, led by Deadly Dench, Lurcher's even more ferocious elder brother, came rocketing down the road, driving straight for the band of tree-savers, who broke up, scattered and ran for safety.

Thomas, helpless and furious, watched from the shelter of the Post Office doorway as they roared back and forth, again and again, accompanied by ear-splitting revs, bangs and shrieks. Finally a police car, summoned by P.C. Spriggs, arrived on the scene and

the 'Angels' sped away to seek further entertainment elsewhere.

Thomas and Blossom emerged from their shelter, clutching their pennants still. All was deserted except for Tamworth Pig and Melanie gazing into each other's eyes, oblivious of the whole world. Thomas and Blossom also stared, Thomas in despair, Blossom beaming from ear to ear.

"Look at them," she breathed.

"I never thought it really happened," Hedgecock grunted. "And I'm very sorry to see it does."

"Love, love, love," Mr. Rab warbled happily.

"Shut up, you stripy fool. Can't you see we're in for trouble? This afternoon has been a failure in every way," Hedgecock said.

"A failure? You mean a disaster," Thomas groaned.

Chapter Four

————————————————— ✳ —————————————————

Next day, the Autumn sunshine had gone at last as the gales roared over the land, blasting the bright flowers, stripping the trees, blustering, whistling, roaring.

"Summer's gone and we've come."

Thomas's thoughts were as stormy as the weather as he sat in the classroom putting the finishing touches to a papier mâché puppet he was making and, ever after, this particular puppet always had to play the villain because of the ferocity of his painted face.

His stomach ached and he wanted to cry but could not. Tamworth had always been there across the years, as long as he could remember, invariably wise and kind and splendid, a true friend. But now he just seemed to be a silly old fool of a pig. How could Tamworth behave like a pop-singing teenager over this little fat pig with nothing whatsoever to recommend her as far as Thomas could see?

Thomas had learnt that grown-ups almost always let you down at some time or another, but not Tamworth. Tamworth was different. All the glorious days, the happy adventures would be gone like a dandelion clock in a puff of wind if he were to start doting on some female. Furthermore, Thomas was convinced that if Tamworth had not been so enraptured by that same black and pink creature, the march would not have been ruined so easily by Deadly Dench and his gang, making fools of all of them.

They had been waiting for him at playtime, cat-calling and gloating, just as he knew they would be, Lurcher Dench and Christopher Robin Baggs and all their mates. Lurcher and Thomas had exchanged a blow each when scuds of rain swept violently across the playground and the whistle blew for them to come in. They had to be content with kicking each other in line, and being reprimanded for doing so.

At lunchtime the storm was so fierce that there was no chance at all of going outside, so they read and drew and played games in the classroom while, all around him, Thomas could hear the whispers.

"We'll get him. We'll finish him. Old Twopenny Tom! Old Measlebug. Tamworth Pig's a silly old fool, they ought to send him back to school. Measlebug. Ugh! Chicken! Thomas is a lemon. Lame dog, Thomas. Chicken! Lame pig. Tamworth. Chicken! Chicken! Don't like it. Don't like it!"

He stuck his fingers in his ears and tried to read but there was no escape. He had no allies. He had gone to school late after a lot of illness, which was why he was known as Measlebug, and he did not make friends easily. He preferred animals. So he was alone against the class, though most of the girls probably would not interfere. Blossom and her friends would come to his aid if they could, but their classroom was on the far side of the school building and they would not be much use against Christopher Robin and his gang, plus Lurcher and his brothers, the school being full of Denches, all tough as old boots.

The afternoon break came after the puppet-making. The wind dropped at last and the clouds lifted for a moment. Play was outside even though the ground was wet with puddles. Thomas stuck his hands in his pockets, his head in the air and swaggered out on to the shiny asphalt. There they were, eleven of them, like a football line-up. They started to shuffle slowly to form a circle around him.

Thomas stood his ground as they approached and then leapt at Lurcher. If he could break him the rest would run. He grabbed the Dench locks and then jabbed to the chin with his left. But the others were now upon him. He managed to hit Christopher Robin right in his spotty face before he fell to the ground beneath a heap of thrusting, punching, hitting, kicking arms and legs. He did not see Henry, the Professor's son, brought up on strict methods of fair play, and horrified at such an unequal battle, rush forward to try to pull a few at least off the prostrate Thomas.

Then, from far away, sounded a fearsome ululation. Blossom's class emerged late from a reluctant Maths lesson, each moment of which was agony for Blossom answering everything wrong, and now, whooping and war-crying, they charged· round the corner like young Amazons.

Encouraged, Thomas managed to squirm his way out of the scrum wriggling around and over him. But, by now, the many Dench brothers, Nosher, Basher,

Prodder and Crasher, had gathered their gangs from their assorted classes and were joyously hurtling into what looked like being the scrap of the year.

Minor battles broke out on the periphery of the main contest which heaved and surged like an enormous, many-tentacled monster in the middle of the playground.

There was little rhyme and less reason in the fighting. Boys hit their pals and girls kicked their best friends. Even the Infants, pouring in from their own playground, hopelessly pursued by a new and gentle helper, were screaming and pulling each other's hair and rolling on the wet ground.

Into the maelstrom strode Mrs. Twitchie, followed by the teacher on duty who had gone to fetch her. She blew her whistle. The heap of bodies disintegrated. Children picked themselves off the ground, then stood rooted to the spot. Mrs. Twitchie wasted no time.

"There will be no playtime tomorrow. The entire school will assemble in the hall and recite prayers instead."

Slowly she scanned the silent figures.

"Who began this fight?"

The finger of Gwendolyn Twitchie, the Headmistress's daughter, pointed at Thomas who stood wet, bruised and bleeding, sweater hanging like seaweed.

"Thomas, you will lose all next week's playtimes. You can come to me each day for a task to do."

He was past caring. All he wanted was a hole where he could hide away. But Blossom cried out in protest, and the measured voice of Henry spoke.

"I do not think that Thomas can be held entirely responsible."

Mrs. Twitchie was above minor interruptions. She waved a hand, the school crawled inside. Silence lay like a blanket save for one whisper.

"Wait till after school. We'll really get you then."

The rest of the afternoon was a blur to Thomas, but at last time for coats and caps and home came. He walked slowly out of the classroom towards the gate. No help there. All the parents waited at the Infant exit round the corner. Thomas walked out of the playground. Yes, there they were, twenty boys at least, perched up on the wall. Out of the corner of his eye, Thomas saw Henry move into step beside him. No

glasses, he thought. They must have been broken. The boys, led by Christopher Robin, jumped down from the wall. Thomas felt sick. He ached all over. Here we go again, he thought, lifting his grazed fists. That's odd. No Lurcher with them. Funny that. Still, makes it easier. Wait for it!

And through the air sounded the click of trotters and the ring of hoofs. Down the road came Tamworth, ears a-prick, tail curled up, every inch the pig of pigs, as a sudden gleam of watery sunshine struck the gold of his skin. Close behind him trotted Joe, the Shire Horse, and Barry MacKenzie Goat. Tamworth's eyes shone with all his old warmth and friendship. He surveyed the band of boys with amused contempt, then turned to Thomas.

"I thought you might be in need of a lift home today, dear boy. Jump up on my back."

Joe was rearing casually in the lane showing his great hoofs, and Barry idly lowered his horns.

"Giddy-up, giddy-up, Tamworth," Thomas yelled, grinning all over his face.

What a glorious world! Being unhappy, being beaten was for other people! Nothing to do with him. He gripped the furry ears.

"Meet my friend. Here he is. He's called Henry. Tamworth, I've got a friend."

The waiting band of boys scattered in the face of such formidable opponents and slunk quietly away to their homes.

Chapter Five

———————————*———————————

"You see," Tamworth said to Blossom and Thomas as they sat in Pig House that evening, "I spent the whole day thinking and I came to the only possible conclusion."

"What's that?" Blossom asked.

"That I must never see Melanie again."

"Oh no!" Blossom cried.

"Very good idea. You don't really want to have anything to do with her, do you? Thomas asked.

"Yes," Tamworth replied.

They sat in silence for a moment.

"I don't hold with females, because they're always causing trouble," Hedgecock muttered. "I don't mean you, Blossom, but then you're not a proper female, are you?"

Blossom glared at him, mouth open with indignation, but Mr. Rab spoke up for her.

"I think Blossom is a delightful female," he said, and bowed a little bow.

"Shut up both of you," Thomas called out. "It doesn't matter whether she's a female or a washing machine. I want to know what Tamworth is going to do."

"I shall work even harder for the cause. I must save the trees. Melanie lives far away up north and will not come back here unless I ask her."

"Why did she come in the first place?" Thomas asked.

"She saw my photograph in the paper and persuaded the farmer's daughter to bring her to see me. But later I heard the farmer was angry with them, as it was a long journey. So that is that. Moreover, I have decided to devote my life to helping my country and domestic happiness has little part therein. Besides. . . ."

His voice quavered a little.

"She is a very young pig, too young for me."

"Oh, poor Tamworth," Blossom cried. "Never mind, you'll still have us."

"Yes, my dear, my very dear friends. We must think of her no more."

He shook himself a little and took a deep breath.

"Now, I want to plan the next march so that it is a real success. No more failures, eh, Thomas?"

Tamworth threw himself heart and soul into his campaign and the next march was splendidly attended. There were no motor bikes wrecking it this time because Tamworth obtained several tickets for a first division football match and contrived that Deadly Dench and his friends received them. He opened bazaars, held meetings and arranged sponsored walks. He spoke on the local television news and soon his campaign gained fame throughout the country. The Vicar's wife made a recording of "Save the Trees", and

it rose to number forty-three on the Top Fifty Records Chart, to the surprise of everyone except Mr. Rab, who thought it should have been number one.

Blossom and Thomas gathered great quantities of acorns, hazel and chestnuts and, every evening, they set off with nut-filled carrier bags to plant as many as possible in ditches, along hedgerows and on any available wasteland.

Thomas collected all the flower pots he could find and set orange and apple pips in them. He placed them in a dark cupboard along with the Christmas hyacinths planted by Mummy. In one of the pots, Mr. Rab planted a tinned strawberry.

"You stupid fool, that will never grow," Hedge-cock snorted.

"Oh yes, it will. I've used a special compost for it. Think of all those beautiful tinned strawberries growing on trees."

Hedgecock rolled over and over, laughing so much that all his feathery prickles got tangled and he had to spend some time grooming himself.

Every day Mr. Rab inspected his little pot to see if the strawberry tree was coming up, but it never did. At last he dug up all the compost and looked for it but, of the strawberry, there was no sign at all.

He had a little weep to Blossom, when Hedgecock was not looking, because he did not want to look like the stripy fool Hedgecock always said he was.

"Never mind. Let's put a conker in a milk bottle with some water and watch it grow," Blossom consoled him.

Meanwhile the festivities of an English Autumn followed their traditional pattern. The Harvest Festival was followed by the Harvest Supper, a huge success, marred only for Thomas by the Vicar bending down from his lean and stately height to inquire how his conker collection was progressing. Thomas found himself incapable of speech. But the Vicar only smiled his austere smile and moved away to talk to someone else.

Hallowe'en was always well celebrated because October 31st was Blossom's birthday. This year she was to have a Fancy Dress party. She had a witch's cloak to wear with a tall hat and a broomstick, while Thomas had a black tracksuit with a luminous skeleton painted on it. Mr. Rab had a velvet coat, for he was to be the witch's cat, and Hedgecock a green toad. Masks were provided for one and all and black balloons with funny faces on them hung from the ceiling.

Thomas spent most of the day at Pig House, once he had inspected Blossom's presents to make sure she had not received something he especially wanted himself. (He was always jealous on Blossom's birthday.) However, only a beautiful set of felt pens aroused his envy, and she promised to lend them to him.

"I wish you'd come to the party, Tamworth," he said.

"I'll come along later to give her my present."

"I gave her a new poetry book," Mr. Rab said proudly.

"You give her one every year," Hedgecock snorted.

"She loves poetry. She liked it much better than your 'History of Numbers through the Ages'."

"I think it's marvellous."

"Maybe it is, to you, but you ought to buy people what they like, not what you like."

Hedgecock hit him hard. Mr. Rab sobbed and hugged himself with his thin paws.

"What a long day," Thomas yawned.

"That's because you're waiting for the party. What time does it begin?" Tamworth asked.

"Five o'clock, so that it will be dark for the games. I shall attack Gwendolyn Twitchie and make her horribly afraid."

He cheered up considerably at the beauty of this thought.

"Is she coming? I thought Blossom didn't like her any more," Tamworth said.

"She wasn't invited at first, but she kicked up such a fuss that Blossom asked her after all. I wouldn't have done."

Five o'clock at last arrived and so did the guests, strangely clean and subdued, clutching parcels. Daddy went out muttering about some important business he had to see to. Mrs. Postlewaithe had come to help Mummy with the food. Jolly good it was too, baked chestnuts and baked potatoes, hot doughnuts and spiced buns, as well as the usual jelly, ice-cream, crisps and lemonade. Lights were turned off, and candles lit in the pumpkins as the guests approached the food, politely at first.

Ten minutes later they looked more their usual selves, with hair and hats falling down, costumes drenched in lemonade or Coca-Cola, and Mrs. Postlewaithe on her hands and knees on the floor picking up abandoned buns and sandwiches.

Birthday cake was to come later, so masks were donned to play the first game, Pass the Parcel. Despite wild cheating and snatching by Thomas, it was won by Gwendolyn Twitchie. Thomas retired to a corner to brood on his revenge. Musical Bumps and Dead Lions followed. Gwendolyn won Dead Lions too.

Seeing Thomas's angry scowls, Mummy decided it would be a good idea to have the moonlight walk in the garden before the fancy dresses fell apart. The children were very excited by this and ran up and down the garden path whooping and playing ghosts. At last, Mrs. Postlewaithe blew a whistle and counted the heads as they came in again.

"It's all right," she said. "Eighteen heads altogether."

"Your Thomas seems to be enjoying himself," she went on, while the children scattered for hide and seek. "He was smiling all over his face."

Mummy was just putting out the birthday cake. She looked surprised.

"That's odd. He usually hates parties, especially girls' parties."

Blossom knew a splendid hiding-place, behind the blankets in the airing cupboard. She wriggled in happily and thought what a wonderful day she was

having. A figure crept in beside her. Oh bother, it's Thomas, she thought. She peered in the gloom. It did not seem like Thomas. As far as she could see it was not anyone she knew at all. She started to tremble and edged forward to push the door open. Light streamed in.

"What's up?" asked the figure.

She knew that voice. Relief made her furious. She stopped trembling.

"Lurcher Dench!" she snapped crossly and pulled off his mask.

"Ow!" he exclaimed as the sharp elastic bit him.

"What are you doing here? I didn't invite you."

"I know. I'm sorry."

Blossom stared at the old enemy. Grey eyes looked pleadingly out of a freckled face.

"You see, I never go to parties. Nobody ever asks me, and Mum never 'as a party. Not with all us lads."

Blossom tried to go on looking angry.

"I like you, Blossom. I like the stories you tell. I'd like you to tell me some, and please, can I stop and 'ave some cake?"

A slow grin spread across her face.

"When did you get in?"

"With the kids in the garden. I made me costume. Look, it's newspaper and I painted it black and joined the rest."

"That's funny. I thought Mum counted us, and Mrs. Postlewaithe definitely did. She must have got it wrong. Come on, let's give up. I want to see Thomas's face when he sees you."

Thomas won the game of Hide and Seek, hidden under a sack of potatoes in the pantry. He came out to receive his prize and saw Lurcher. Stiff with rage he stalked over to him.

"Outside," he hissed, jerking his thumb.

"Don't go. I'm just going to blow out the candles and cut the cake," Blossom cried, but they completely ignored her as they marched to the door in their newspaper and skeleton outfits.

Mummy came in from the kitchen.

"Come on, Blossom. What are you waiting for?"

She hesitated for a moment, then blew out the candles. Whatever happened, food was always a great comfort.

Thomas and Lurcher took up their positions on the lawn and fought long and silently in the dark and the cold, oblivious of the singing and laughter inside. They were alone for the first time, their battle uncomplicated by interfering adults, allies or spectators, the issue straightforward at last, Thomas or Lurcher.

They were well matched, Lurcher the heavier, Thomas faster. Lurcher stronger but Thomas fiercer. They struck and danced away, weaving, dodging and punching in the moonlight. Thomas fought for his own territory and Lurcher fought for the right to enter Blossom's world of stories, games and campaigns.

At last they broke and fell back, battered, exhausted but satisfied, all hatred gone, the result a draw. The lawn was littered with the shreds of the newspaper costume.

They entered the room arm in arm and advanced for their share of the cake. Parents were arriving to take away the guests. Mummy was handing each one a lollipop when her eyes alighted on the battle-marked pair. Swiftly she pushed them into the kitchen.

"I'll deal with you later," she said grimly.

They sat with quiet resignation awaiting her return. After a while, Thomas found a cold flannel for his bleeding mouth and handed Lurcher a dishcloth for his swollen eye. They listened to the noise of those departing. This noise crescendoed enormously.

"That sounds like Mrs. Twitchie," Lurcher remarked.

Thomas tried to grin despite his painful lips.

"I'd forgotten," he said.

"Forgotten what?"

"I locked Gwendolyn in the shed when we went round the garden and I forgot to let her out."

"That's why Ma Postlewaithe didn't spot me when she counted us in."

Voices and footsteps came near. Angry voices, hard steps. United they turned to meet their doom.

But later, when all the telling off was over and Mrs. Twitchie and Gwendolyn had finally gone, Blossom was waiting with two vast slices of cake and lollipops for all the Dench children.

Chapter Six

*

Half-term arrived and, on one fine afternoon, Blossom, Thomas, Tamworth, Hedgecock and Mr. Rab set off for the Tumbling Wood. Mr. Rab's nose was a-twitch with excitement at the prospect of visiting the Welsh Rabbit once more.

Thomas carried a bag to collect sweet chestnuts, this time, for the year's crop was a record one and they lay on the ground in thousands just waiting to be picked up. Never had there been such a time for nuts. The squirrels had filled every nest and every secret cache and still the woods were carpeted with them.

Sweet chestnut cases are very prickly, and hands and paws grew sore as they picked up one after another, cracking the outer shells to reveal the brown nuts curled inside, three of them, unlike the single conker.

At last, the bag full, they stopped, content. Six hundred and thirty-one nuts Hedgecock reported, a pleasant addition to the food Tamworth and Blossom had brought with them. They both believed that food improved all occasions.

They left Mr. Rab by the elderberry bush so that he could see his friend, then rambled on to the centre of the wood.

"Let's eat something, I'm starving," Blossom said.

"Wait until we find the right place," Thomas answered.

"How do we know when it is the right place?"

"I shall know when I see it," he said, running along the path with Hedgecock. Tamworth and Blossom followed more slowly, thinking about food.

Suddenly he turned sharply right, straight up the wooded hill.

"There's a path here. Come on!" he called.

"I cannot perceive any sign whatsoever of a path, dear boy," Tamworth puffed.

"Nor me," Blossom agreed.

This was not surprising, as she was quietly investigating the picnic bag to see if she could sneak a chocolate biscuit without anyone noticing.

"I think I got the number right," Hedgecock was muttering to himself. "I think it was six hundred and thirty-one, not six hundred and twenty-three."

Thomas ran ahead up the slope, brushing aside nettles and brambles.

"Look, somebody's cut steps here."

Between the moss and the fallen leaves, the edge of a stone step showed. On and up they climbed, Thomas now far ahead, almost seeming to fly. The others stumbled after, scratched and nettled and not at all eager.

At last Thomas stopped and the others caught up with him. A great ring of giant beech trees loomed up against the sky at the summit of the hill. Within this ring stretched a smooth, green lawn, all soft, springy

grass, clear of nettles or bracken. Right in the centre
stood a tree of immense girth, the widest tree they had
ever seen, with powerful branches growing almost

horizontally from the trunk. They ran to it and tried to encircle it, but they could not.

"It makes you look small, Tamworth," Thomas shouted.

"It's a British Oak, the finest tree in the world. It takes three hundred years to grow, three hundred years to live, three hundred years to die and a hundred years to fall down."

"That's a thousand years," Hedgecock breathed in delight.

"Oh, do let's eat here. I love this place. Mr. Rab would say that it was enchanted," Blossom exclaimed.

"Silly old fool. I'm glad he isn't here or he'd be going on about fairies," Hedgecock replied.

They laid an old groundsheet on the short turf and sat down. Soon all was silent save for the sound of eating. At the bottom of the bag, Thomas found a paper flag left over from summer days. He put it in his pocket, climbed on to Tamworth's back and managed to haul himself on to the lowest branch. There he fixed his flag, a Union Jack.

"My tree," he remarked as he descended.

"Our tree," Blossom corrected him.

"The tree of Saint Thomas."

Blossom did not bother to reply. Sometimes it just was not worth arguing with Thomas. But she thought to herself that it would always be the king of the wood for her.

At last they decided to go home, turning at the ring of beech trees for one last look at the noble oak. They could just see Thomas's little flag.

"You know, that tree might have been growing when William the Conqueror invaded the land," Tamworth said.

He looked thoughtful.

"For me, it seems to stand for all the trees in the country."

Mr. Rab was waiting for them beside the elderberry bush. He was very excited and would not listen when they tried to tell him about the oak tree. He was full of his own news.

"My friend the Welsh Rabbit says there's trouble coming to this wood. All the wild animals are full of strange rumours. More and more machines are arriving and men in bowler hats pop up everywhere."

"We haven't seen any machines today," Tamworth said.

"There are six on the other side of the wood, he says."

Tamworth looked grave.

"I have a feeling the wood is in danger. It is going to need our campaign."

Chapter Seven

*

Late that night the wind rose and howled loudly. Towards dawn it reached an absolute pitch of fury, shrieking and whistling wildly. People awoke and got up, unable to sleep again as tiles and slates flew off roofs, garage doors banged and blew in, dustbin lids clashed and clanged in back yards, and fences collapsed like broken matchboxes.

The cricket pavilion was lifted over the hedge and whirled into the pond of the next field. Two of the Vicarage chimney pots were toppled off. Lights were switched on one by one, then went off simultaneously as a line was blown down and the power failed.

Mr. Baggs went round his farm to see that all the animals were safe. Last of all he called into Pig House to visit Tamworth, who was wide awake, staring out of his window at the wild storm-tossed world outside.

"The wind's not doing your trees any good, Tamworth. Branches are falling everywhere. There'll be a lot of damage by morning."

Tamworth turned to Farmer Baggs and sighed.

"It's a sad sight, a sad sight."

"You all right, then, Tamworth?"

"Oh yes. I'm all right. Thank you for calling to see me."

He turned back to the window.

"Lost a bit of weight, 'ee 'ave, Tamworth," Farmer Baggs said, eyeing him.

"Yes, I have. I am somewhat smaller round my middle, I regret to say."

"I'll send 'ee a fresh lot of cabbages, tomorrow. We can't 'ave 'ee getting thin. 'T would never do."

"Thank you, kind friend. I do seem to have lost my appetite lately."

"Well, we'll soon back 'ee up. Try and get some sleep, now, mind. Goodnight, Tamworth."

"Goodnight, Farmer Baggs."

The farmer closed the door behind him and the wind blew louder than ever.

"Summat's wrong with that pig," he muttered to himself as he staggered back to the house, buffeted and beaten by wayward gusts, blowing from all directions.

In his bed, Thomas wrapped Num carefully around Hedgecock and Mr. Rab. They had all been awake for a long time. Mr. Rab trembled pitifully as he listened to the ferocious roar.

"I keep imagining that raggetty men pretending to be leaves are dancing with the wind," he wailed. "They've got mean, pointed faces and they're coming to fetch me, to take me into the cold, dark night and I'm afraid."

He hid his nose, pale with terror, in Num's soft folds.

170

"Raggetty stuffed vegetables! All we have to worry about is if the roof blows off," Hedgecock snapped.

Mr. Rab wailed again.

"I do hope my friend the Welsh Rabbit is safe. Fancy being in a wood on a night like this."

"Oh, he's all right. They're used to roughing it out there. Come on, let's recite a few multiplication tables to cheer ourselves up. There's nothing like the seven times to give one a bit of comfort."

Once more Mr. Rab wailed.

"Oh no, I can't think of anything less comfortable than the seven times table except the eighth or the ninth."

But Thomas also thought tables a good idea and he and Hedgecock had reached eleven times nine is ninety-nine when Mummy opened the door, bearing a candle in an old brass candlestick. She straightened the bed and tucked them all in.

"I'll leave the candle on the chest. It's quite safe and it's a pretty light. I think the wind will die down soon."

At that moment, the most tremendous noise of all was heard, like ten trains crashing. Every window in the house rattled and Mr. Rab shot right down the bed to Thomas's feet in terror.

"What was that?" Blossom cried, rushing in.

She had slept soundly up to then, to be awoken by this most monstrous of sounds.

"I don't know," Mummy said.

Daddy loomed large in the doorway.

"I think it's the elm tree in the village fallen at last. I thought it would, one day. Elm trees have shallow roots and often fall in gales. One tree you couldn't save, Thomas."

"Now off to sleep, everyone. I'm pretty sure the worst is over," Mummy added.

Everyone went to see the tree the next day. It had fallen at an angle down the road, and fortunately no houses were damaged. It looked defenceless with its roots snatched out of the ground.

"Poor tree," Blossom said.

Later, with the branches lopped off and the trunk sawn up, it made a huge bonfire for Guy Fawkes Night. Blossom and Thomas were not very keen on November the Fifth, because all their animal friends hated it so. However, this year, they went to watch

the tree burn in a tremendous fire in a field loaned by
Farmer Baggs.

At school, pictures were painted and poems written

about the fire. Blossom's picture, all black and scarlet and yellow, went up on the wall. Thomas's poem was read out to his class.

> *"Tree growing to the sky,*
> *Flames flowing to the sky,*
> *So did it live,*
> *So did it die."*

"Very good," commented Mr. Starling, their teacher, who was keen on poetry.

Thomas did not tell him that Mr. Rab had made it up in bed the night before the bonfire.

Lurcher Dench's work was read out too, for the first time ever.

> *"I like to see the big bonfire*
> *I like to see the rockets.*
> *Mrs. Twitchie says we mustn't*
> *Have bangers in our pockets."*

Blossom heard all the Denches read in the dinner-hour now. Led by a determined Lurcher, they would appear with their reading books. After she had listened to them read, she would tell them one of her own stories. They listened to every word, the Denches now being as fiercely keen on reading as on fighting.

A strange quiet hung over the school, in fact. Christopher Robin, spotty as ever, walked around with Gwendolyn Twitchie. Only occasionally did Thomas, peacefully racing cars with his friend Henry, regret the old warfare, the joy of battle.

"We're getting soppy," he complained to Tamworth.

"And a good thing too, dear boy. Violence is always to be deplored."

"What's deplored?" Thomas asked.

"I deplore Hedgecock," Mr. Rab said.

"Not half as much as I deplore you," Hedgecock snarled, kicking him hard.

Chapter Eight

———————————— * ————————————

A Jumble Sale was to be held in the School Hall for the Save the Trees campaign funds. Tamworth was going to be there so that people could guess his weight, and a huge cake was the prize for the most accurate estimate. Blossom had promised to help Mummy at a stall, selling old coats, hats and suits.

Thomas went with them most reluctantly. He loathed Jumble Sales, hating everything about them, the smell of old clothes, the frantic rush bearing down on the stalls when the doors opened, the Vicar speaking to him, and Mummy and Blossom gossiping to people he could hardly bear to be in the same room with.

A boy in Blossom's class was disposing of his Matchbox series of cars, so he bought as many of these as he could afford, then mooched around the hall, hands stuffed in pockets, face scowling. He purchased a toffee apple, but could not finish it, so he threw it away behind the piano, and looked up to find the Vicar towering over him. He picked it up hastily, contemplated the dust it had now acquired and walked round trying to find a place to dump it.

"Humph. Fancy, with all this rotten old rubbish everywhere, you can't even get rid of a toffee apple," he muttered.

Finally, he dropped it in his mother's shopping basket. She looked up.

"Thomas, please stay and help at this stall for a moment. I simply must speak to the Vicar's wife. I shan't be long."

"What do I do?" he asked desperately.

"Just take the money they give you for the clothes and put it in this tin. Blossom will help you with the change."

"I can do it better than she can, the stupid, fat nit."

"All right, then. I'll only be a moment. Oh, and do watch your language, Thomas. People don't always like your rude way of talking."

"I shan't speak at all then," he grumbled.

He noticed, crossly, that Mrs. Twitchie and Gwendolyn were selling cakes at the next stall.

"Bet that lot are poisonous," he thought aloud.

People came to the stall, picked up garments and handed him money. He put it in the tin. It grew very hot, so he took off his anorak. Mummy seemed to be gone a long time, but he was doing quite well. One or two people were obviously pleased with their bargains. He was getting into the swing of it when Mummy appeared.

"Thank you, Thomas. I'm sorry I was so long."

"I did very well. I got fifty pence for one coat. Can I go now?"

"Yes. Tell Daddy I'll be coming soon."

He had almost reached the door, encountering a crowd of new arrivals, when a clear voice rang out.

"That woman is wearing my coat!"

It was a voice accustomed to command, the voice of
Mrs. Twitchie. Thomas watched her run across the
hall and seize the arm of a large woman wearing a
blue sheepskin coat. It looked familiar, somehow.

"I've just bought it," came the equally loud voice of
Mrs. Dench, also accustomed to instant obedience.

All the fighting Denches took after her, not Dad,
who was small and silent, and never worked.

"You can't have done. It's not for sale. I only took
it off for a moment. Give it to me."

"Yes, it was. I gave fifty pence for it. That's a lot at a
Jumble Sale, but it's a good coat."

"Of course it is. I gave fifty pounds for it," Mrs. Twitchie cried.

People began to gather round. This was very interesting. Then Thomas remembered suddenly and clearly. His bargain! He'd sold the coat to Mrs. Dench. He tried to edge his way through the throng to escape outside.

"I bought it from the stall. I paid for it and I'm keeping it."

By now the Denches had all gathered round their Mum. She drew herself up to her full height, looming over Mrs. Twitchie, who was going red down her neck with fury. She leaned forward and started to undo the buttons, which only just fastened anyway. Mrs. Dench pulled the edges together again.

"And that's my duffle," Gwendolyn shrieked, pointing at Lurcher, who certainly looked smarter than usual.

The Vicar and his wife now came forward.

"I'm sure we can solve this problem. Is this Mrs. Twitchie's coat, my dear?"

"Yes, I think so."

"Of course it is," Mrs. Twitchie bellowed.

She was not used to having her word doubted. The Vicar patted her arm. She pushed him off.

"You've got to do something," she snapped.

"Mrs. Dench, you must see that this is all a mistake. We'll gladly refund the money. Which stall was it?"

The Vicar was trying hard to keep the peace.

"Mrs. Thingummy's," Mrs. Dench said, pointing

at Mummy's stall. "That small boy Timothy sold it to me."

She could never remember her own children's names, let alone anyone else's.

Silence fell as heads turned to the stall, then searched round the hall for Thomas. Frantically he tried to push his way out. Mummy had gone very pink.

"I'm sorry. I shouldn't have left Thomas here. He must have sold it."

Blossom, weeping, flung her arms round her.

"It's not my Mummy's fault," she cried.

"We all know whose fault it is. Thomas, come here!"

Mrs. Twitchie's stentorian tones filled the hall.

Thomas turned blindly, hemmed in by people, who stared at him, pushing him forward. He could not get his breath. Panic rose in him. All these horrible people! And he had not meant it. It was not fair, she must have left her coat near the stall. He had only tried to help.

Something soft thrust into his hand. It was Tamworth's snout. The crowd fell back at last as the huge pig moved to his friend.

"Up, Thomas. Get on my back, old lad."

He pulled himself on to the familiar, golden back as the deep voice rang out, drowning the angry splutters of Mrs. Dench and Mrs. Twitchie.

"Friends," Tamworth cried, "let us not make fools of ourselves. Let us be calm and sensible. Thomas, my dear friend here, made a mistake. Well, which of us has never made a mistake? We all have made mistakes. And, by the way, that's Thomas's anorak you're wearing, Crasher Dench. You see, Mrs. Twitchie, Thomas was quite fair. He sold his own clothes, too."

The crowd laughed. The Vicar smiled his austere smile.

"Come, Mrs. Dench. Give Mrs. Twitchie her coat. Your money and our apologies shall be given to you."

The clothes were handed back, the money returned.

"Furthermore," Tamworth said blandly, his voice like cream, "Mrs. Dench has guessed my weight correctly and so has won the cake, which, I'm sure, will be appreciated by her admirable family."

Mrs. Dench looked astonished, as well she might, never having bought a ticket to guess Tamworth's weight. Then she smiled.

"Thank you, Tamworth."

"Thank you, madam. And thank you, Mrs. Twitchie, for your kind forgiveness of us all."

Mrs. Twitchie was still glowering alternately at Thomas and the Denches.

Never one to lose an opportunity, Tamworth concluded, "Thank you, everyone. Remember our cause, and come to the next march. Save the trees!"

"Save the trees!" re-echoed through the hall. The Vicar's wife began to sing.

"Shush, my dear," the Vicar said.

She stopped singing.

Mummy went up to Mrs. Dench and said quietly, "Let Crasher keep the anorak. I think he likes it."

The entertainment was over, so the crowd moved on. Thomas stroked Tamworth's ears and slid off his back. Lurcher Dench pulled his arm, his eyes like slits.

"We don't want your manky old clothes."

They glared at one another and together pushed their way outside to the field behind the hall.

Lurcher kicked Thomas's shin. Thomas punched him on his nose.

"That's better," he panted almost happily, as they fell to the ground pummelling each other.

Life was back to normal again. Tamworth would disapprove, Mummy would grumble, but Thomas knew that when he and Lurcher were fighting each other, everything was all right.

Chapter Nine

✳

At first Tamworth would not believe the news, then, gradually, he realized that it must be true. He looked at the two small forms, both hanging on his words, expecting him to think of the solution to their problems, then and there.

"You say that the motorway is going to by-pass the village, which we knew, but that, instead of going east through the slag heaps, where we thought it would go, and where it would only improve the landscape, it is being directed straight through Tumbling Wood, so that the hill will be levelled and all the wood destroyed. Is that it, my friend?"

"Yes, indeed to goodness," the Welsh Rabbit replied. "From all directions reports are coming in, they are, man."

He lowered his voice.

"Some do say that the Minister of Environment has been all over the woods, himself in person."

"We've met Ministers before," Mr. Rab quavered. "They're nothing to Tamworth."

He tried to snap his paws but failed lamentably. He was very nervous. Tamworth perceived that he had described his friends to the Welsh Rabbit as being very clever and important and he was anxious that they should live up to this. But the Welsh Rabbit did not look as if he were easily impressed.

"Mr. Rab, my friend here, said that you got things done, that you had influence, man. That's why the animals in the wood sent me to see you, to stop this terrible thing, this threat to our lives and our homes."

Tamworth looked grave.

"I don't think that I've the sort of influence that moves motorways. Besides, I like motorways. I think they will solve traffic problems and bring prosperity, but that we must be sure they take the best path through the countryside."

He sat back on his haunches and brooded for a while. Mr. Rab twitched and wriggled, but managed to keep silent for once. At last Tamworth spoke.

"I think this is all we can do. First, write to the Minister and find out definitely if the motorway is to go through the wood. Second, if so, we must get up a petition asking if the original route can be used instead. Third, promote publicity about the wood and its beauty. It's not very well known at present. Fourth, carry on with our 'Save the Trees' campaign."

He reflected for a moment.

"Plans have been changed, though not often. Let us hope, my friends, that this will be one of those rare successes."

"Thank you, Tamworth the Pig. I see what they are saying, you are indeed a clever pig, and we shall

in your trotters leave it. I will tell the wood dwellers
that you are trying to save them. Or else at the worst
it is, we have all lost our homes."

"Indeed to goodness, yes," Mr. Rab agreed.

So began the biggest campaign ever. Blossom and
Thomas drew poster after poster. Tamworth, getting
steadily thinner, held meetings and toured the countryside on Farmer Baggs's tractor, speaking through a
loud hailer. He went into school and addressed the
children. Mrs. Twitchie was most polite, for Tamworth as a Very Important Pig was quite different from
Tamworth, friend of terrible Thomas.

Next day the children were all gathered together in
the school garden. Mrs. Twitchie, wearing a mackin-
tosh and gumboots, emerged with Mr. Starling following. He carried a small sapling and a spade. Mrs
Twitchie's clarion tones rang out.

"Children! I am about to plant a tree!"

She took the spade from Mr. Starling and dug into
the ground. There was a clink as it struck a stone.

Thomas watched with mixed feelings. He wanted to
save trees, especially the Tumbling Wood trees, very
much indeed, but he hated being on the same side as
Mrs. Twitchie. He started to wriggle. He wanted to
kick Christopher Robin Baggs, standing just in front
of him, but Blossom slid in quietly beside him. She
knew how he felt.

"Tamworth says we have to use all the support we
can get when it's a Cause, even if it's someone we don't
like," she whispered.

So Thomas stood still, while Mrs. Twitchie, tired of

digging, handed over the spade for Mr. Starling to finish the job. A cheer went up as the tree was finally planted. Thomas tried to join in but he could not, and was saved by a gusty shower of rain splattering over them, speeding them all back to the classrooms.

Meanwhile the Vicar's wife knitted sweaters with "Save the Trees" on the front. These proved popular

and soon all the children were wearing them. Lurcher Dench liked his very much. He had not had a new sweater for ages. A famous firm got to hear of them and bought the pattern from her for a large sum of money, and hundreds of sweaters were made in their factories. With this and the money from her record, she became quite rich. However, the Vicar did not like this at all and made her give most of the money away to charity. She did buy a beautiful red velvet dress, though. Mummy went with her to choose it.

Tamworth wrote to a badge manufacturer and soon thousands of green and gold "Save the Trees" badges were being worn on tee-shirts throughout the length and breadth of the land, as their owners went out to plant nuts, pips and seeds in all sorts of likely and un-likely places from quiet lanes to cracks and crevices in concrete yards.

Tamworth was asked to appear on "This Week in England", a television programme.

Thomas brushed him and scratched his back.

"Shall I shampoo you like I did before, when you went on television?"

"No, not that again," Tamworth said, shuddering at the memory of it. "The water was icy."

"I know," Thomas said, and shot away to return with a large tin of talcum powder which he up-ended over Tamworth.

"Atishoo! Atishoo!" Tamworth trumpeted, now a white not a golden pig.

He looked at himself in the Pig House mirror and groaned.

"I look like the ghost of a pig."

But Thomas brushed so firmly and steadily that Tamworth's coat emerged, shining and clean, though a slightly paler shade of gold.

"That's better. By the time the make-up girls have finished with me, I shan't look too bad."

Suddenly he looked sad.

"But I am not the Pig I was, you know, Thomas, I'm much too thin."

"You're all right. I know, smoke your new pipe in between questions. It will give you the right air."

Tamworth's television appearance went off well and the number of visitors to the Tumbling Wood increased tenfold.

"Beauty Spot In Danger—Pig Speaks" ran the headline in a famous daily newspaper.

But one evening, when Blossom was returning home from a music lesson, she found Joe the Shire Horse waiting for her.

"I want a word with 'ee, Blossom," he said in his slow way.

"Yes, Joe. What's it all about?"

She felt in her anorak pocket for a lump of sugar. She found two, and they both crunched together.

"It be about Tamworth."

"What about him?"

"Well, 'ee don't laugh no more and 'ee don't sleep. Night after night 'ee's up and down Pig 'ouse."

"He's very busy saving the trees."

"It ain't only that. He sits dreaming for hours, reciting bits o' poetry."

"He's always recited poetry."

"Not love poetry! And worst of all, 'ee's getting so thin."

"Yes, lots of people have noticed. They keep writing to him, asking if he's on a diet and can he recommend one. But Tamworth doesn't want to be thin. Well, Joe, what do you think is wrong?"

Joe bent his head low and whispered in her ear. She nodded.

"Yes, yes. I'll see to it. I really will. I'll do all I can, Joe, I promise."

So Blossom went home to make inquiries and to write letters that had nothing whatsoever to do with saving trees or moving motorways.

Chapter Ten

---- * ----

Daddy piled a great deal of marmalade on to his toast and reached out for the Sunday papers with a sigh of satisfaction. He turned to the sports page, then fixed an irritable eye on Blossom.

"What are you tittering about?"

"You dropped a chunk of marmalade in your tea."

He arose, stalked to the kitchen, tipped the tea down the sink, returned and poured out another cup, then sat down and reached for his newspaper, holding it up firmly between Blossom and himself. A minute passed peacefully.

"Daddy," she cried.

"Oh! For heaven's sake, what's the matter now?"

"Look at that."

"At what? England's doing well in Australia."

"No, no. Look at this page. Here."

"I wish you wouldn't read the paper when I do."

"But look, please."

"What at?"

" 'Mrs. Baggs Speaks. Exclusive Interview. Pig is wrong, she says.' "

Daddy found the place and continued aloud.

" 'In an interview with our reporter, Mrs. Baggs stroked her curls' . . ."

"What, those greasy sausages?" Thomas interrupted.

" 'and talked to us in her beautiful farmhouse.' "

"You mean that smelly old dump."

" ' "Tamworth Pig is a threat to our country," she said. "He hinders progress and ruins the morals of the young" ' . . ."

"What's morals?" Thomas asked.

"Goodness and things. Oh, never mind. Let me go on. ' "He's big-headed and pig-headed," ' she continued, looking every inch a farmer's wife' . . ."

"And there's hundreds of inches of her," Thomas shouted.

". . . ' "I have treated that pig like my own child, and I have received nothing but ingratitude and unkind words. I fed him with my own hands and the finest food" ' . . ."

"I hope she kept them separate," Mummy put in.

". . . ' "and so he started his Grow More Food campaign and spoke against me" ' . . ."

"Oh, how can she tell such lies?" Blossom breathed.

". . . ' "Mrs. Baggs, what do you think of his latest campaign to save Tumbling Wood," our reporter asked. "It's a shame and a disgrace. The wood is an eyesore, full of rotting trees and rubbish that has been dumped there" ' . . ."

"If there's any rubbish, she must have put it there. I bet she would too, the old ratbag."

"Thomas!" Mummy said in a horrified voice.

Daddy lowered the paper.

"Loyalty to your friends should not affect your language, Thomas. By the way, I think Mrs. Baggs's brother Bert is a sub-contractor to the firm building the motorway, which may account for her attitude."

He read on.

" 'Our reporter then said that he believed that Farmer Baggs was very fond of Tamworth Pig. "He's a gentle, kind man, Mr. Baggs is, and he cannot see the villainy that is in such a wicked animal as that pig, but, in time, we shall all see," she concluded.' "

Thomas was drumming with his heels, his face bright crimson.

"I'm going to kill her," he said.

"You mustn't talk like that, Thomas. It does no good," Mummy reproved him.

"I'm off to take it to Tamworth," Thomas said.

"Tamworth has all the Sunday newspapers anyway, so he won't need this one. Don't worry about him, he'll know what to do," Daddy replied.

In fact, Tamworth treated the whole thing as a joke and was especially polite to Mrs. Baggs when she appeared with his food as usual, a smirk in the corners of her mouth.

But Thomas spent the day in a state of fury, planning revenges, none of which seemed likely to succeed. It was no use kidnapping her or emptying Tamworth's food over her head. He did think of putting on his skeleton costume and hiding in her wardrobe so that he could jump out at her when she had gone to bed, but it really did not seem practicable.

What he did do, in the end, was to waylay Christopher Robin Baggs, seize him by his bow tie, force him

down on his knees, and compel him to say that Tamworth Pig was the greatest.

Christopher Robin squirmed and tears ran down his cheeks, but afterwards he told Mrs. Twitchie about it, so Thomas came off worse after all. He was barred from football until the end of term because of his lack of sportsmanship.

After school, he sat bitterly beside Tamworth under the damson tree.

"It's not fair," he said.

"I told you violence is wrong," Tamworth murmured to him, rubbing his snout against him. "We must be patient and bide our time, Thomas."

"I don't like patience and biding. I like fighting and winning," Thomas said with great conviction.

Chapter Eleven

————————————— ✳ —————————————

It was the Welsh Rabbit, on swiftly flying paws, who brought the news to Mr. Rab.

"The campaign has failed. Bulldozers have up the wood started to tear."

Blossom and Thomas rushed to Tamworth and five minutes later he was riding through the village on Farmer Baggs's tractor, calling through a loud-speaker to a rapidly gathering audience.

"Brothers! Friends! A cry for help has sounded. We must help our brothers the trees and those who live in their shelter. Without warning, the machines are moving in to destroy the prettiest spot in the whole country. Come, let us to the wood. Let us save the trees!"

A ragged cheer arose. Tamworth held up a trotter.

"Forward, my friends. To the wood!"

Children rushed away, to return with flags and banners, and set off behind Tamworth, Blossom and Thomas. Hedgecock and Mr. Rab climbed up on Joe's back. The students appeared, being ever on the alert for a demonstration, and animals and birds came running and flying. Rather more slowly, the grown-ups joined in the procession, one at a time, at first, then in twos and threes until they were pouring out of their houses, rallied by the Vicar's wife's voice ringing through the air.

> *"Save the Trees,*
> *Save the Trees,*
> *We're marching over there to save the trees!"*

Lurcher ran up beside Joe.

"We're with you on this," he shouted to the un-welcoming face of Thomas who had climbed on Joe's back. "Deadly's coming to help, too."

"You'd better," Thomas snarled, then lent a hand to haul him up.

The roar of motor bikes was heard as the leather-jackets formed an escort to the procession.

P.C. Cubbins and P.C. Spriggs ran out, but they could only go along with the steadily increasing throng.

"Forward!" Tamworth cried. "It is the Cause!"

More and more people joined in. Cars and Land-Rovers bumped along the track as folks from out-lying farms and houses enrolled.

> *"Save the Trees,*
> *Save the Trees."*

The cry seemed to rise up to the sky.

"Tamworth," Thomas shouted. "Tam—worth. Tam—worth."

"Tam—worth. Tam—worth. Tam—worth," took up the crowd.

Blossom felt wild excitement rising within her. She

felt like flying, like crying. This was living. This was life. This was better than anything that had ever happened. This was the way to the stars. People were wonderful. People could do anything, save anything. She felt proud. She felt she had wings, a crown on her head, a fire in her heart. She looked at Thomas and Lurcher, loving them. And their eyes were bright and wild, their faces red. She looked at everyone around and behind her, and saw flushed, singing faces, with no sense in any of them. The excitement left her and Blossom was afraid.

"Joe, Joe," she cried in his ear. "Let me down. Let me down. I must see Tamworth."

He paused a moment and she slid off. The crowd pressed up behind and she felt terrified. Now there was no stopping, only going on. Somehow she got up to the tractor.

"Tamworth," she called.

The tractor slowed down and she climbed on to it.

"Tamworth! Oh, Tamworth. I don't like it. They're all mad. Someone will get hurt."

She pulled at him. She wanted to see his face. He turned to her. Tamworth's eyes were as kind and calm as Mummy's were when she told bedtime stories.

"Don't let them . . ." she started.

"It's all right, dear Blossom. No one will get hurt. There will be no violence."

"Are you sure?"

"I promise," said Tamworth Pig.

The wood came into sight.

"There they are," the crowd roared. "The machines.

196

There are the machines. Wreck them! Wreck them!"

Blossom looked at the earth-movers and shuddered.

"Oh, Tamworth. What are we doing?" she whispered.

The crowd was moving rapidly now, shouting, calling, singing, booing. "Save the trees! Wreck the machines!"

"Stop," Tamworth called.

The crowd stopped. Cars and bikes braked erratically. There was a terrible roar like a tide surging on a storm-ridden beach.

"Quiet," Tamworth said.

There was silence. Tamworth spoke, his voice gentle as a summer breeze.

"Brothers and friends. We are here to save, not to destroy, to conserve, not to ruin. We come with love, not hate. Let there be no talk of wrecking. I will speak to the men of the machines."

He drove the tractor forward to the foremost bulldozer. The driver was dark and angry.

"Get those lunatics out of here. We've got a job to do. Out of the way!"

Tamworth held up a trotter.

"I would not stop any man doing his job. I only ask you to wait for a time. I think the plans may be altered, so please don't destroy this wood."

The dark, angry one, glowered.

"Get that lot out of here. Come on, men!"

The machines turned towards the wood.

Tamworth's voice boomed like a jet plane.

"Save the trees!"

Like a huge cloud settling on a mountain top, people and animals surged forward and lay down in the path of the bulldozers. They wrapped themselves round the trees and stayed there. Blossom caught sight of the Vicar's wife lowering her long form to curl round a beech tree and Mr. Rab scurrying away to the elderberry bush. Thomas climbed up beside her. The motor bikes lay scattered on the ground.

"We are prepared to stay here day and night," Tamworth announced calmly.

"Till nine o' clock anyway. I got a date wiv a bird, then," Deadly yelled.

A ginger-haired man dropped down from his earth-mover.

"I'm off home," he said. "I haven't had a Saturday off in weeks. Best of luck, folks. It's a nice wood."

The others followed suit, till only the dark, angry one remained. At last he spoke.

"I'll go. But I'll have you for this, pig!"

The crowd got up slowly to return home to television and Saturday tea. Tamworth and Blossom turned to one another and smiled.

The Welsh Rabbit emerged cautiously with Mr. Rab and Hedgecock.

"A narrow squeak, indeed to goodness," he sighed.

"And Mr. Rab's a narrow pipsqueak," Hedgecock snorted, laughing at his own joke.

Chapter Twelve

───────────────── * ─────────────────

Tamworth sat outside the "Duck and Drake", talking to certain officials and reporters about the proposed new route that the motorway should take. The bulldozers and earth-movers had been halted while various important and high-up personages decided what to do.

Several of Tamworth's friends were there, and refreshment was laid on, beer and cheese and pickled onions from the inn, or coffee and biscuits from the Vicar's wife.

"Yes, I'm expecting a telegram from the Minister at any time now," Tamworth said. "He promised to send one as soon as a decision was reached."

Tamworth looked very pale and his eyes were dull. His ears hung heavily. He nibbled at an apple without enthusiasm.

"Where's Blossom? She's not here. In fact, I haven't seen her all week."

"Oh, she's up to something. She's got that I-know-something-you-don't look on her face. I kicked her yesterday because of it, the silly, fat thing," Thomas said.

"You're horribly mean to Blossom," Mr. Rab protested. "I think she's the nicest girl in the world."

"And I think she's the stupidest," Thomas replied.

A telegraph boy came along the road on his red bicycle.

"Here comes the telegram," Tamworth said.

A Land-Rover was also coming from the other direction with Blossom waving from the front seat, but Tamworth's eyes were fixed on the telegraph boy, who seemed to have developed a puncture, for he had dismounted and was gazing solemnly at his front tyre. Some people ran forward to meet him, but Mr. Rab had been watching the Land-Rover.

He called out excitedly. "It's Blossom! And Farmer Baggs! They're getting out. And there's someone else with them. Oh! Oh! Oh! It's Melanie. It's Melanie. It's love."

Out of the Land-Rover, Blossom beaming at her side, came the pretty little black and pink pig, her plump form wobbling delightfully as she trotted straight towards Tamworth, who sat motionless as if he had been struck by lightning.

A reporter was rushing towards Tamworth, pulling the telegraph boy with him, but the pig had no eyes for them. His ears had pricked up, his eyes were shining and his bristles sparkled. Blossom ran to him and threw her arms round him.

"I had to fetch her. You were so thin and unhappy. I wrote to her farmer and he wrote to Farmer Baggs and then we went to fetch her. Oh, Tamworth, I'm so happy."

"Open the telegram. See what it says! Come on!"

Everyone was milling around Tamworth, who was gazing into Melanie's eyes and gulping.

"I'm too old for you. You want a handsome, young pig."

"You're the handsomest and cleverest pig in the whole world. I want you, and I'm not going away again. Never!"

She turned to Thomas.

"And I know you're Tamworth's friend and please, oh, please, Thomas, please like me."

She put out a black trotter on Thomas's arm and looked at him with her round, black snout and bright eyes. A grin spread slowly over his face.

"I love you," carolled Mr. Rab falling at her feet.

"It might work out," Hedgecock sniffed. "But for pity's sake READ THAT TELEGRAM!"

Tamworth's trotters were trembling wildly, so Blossom opened the envelope. He read it, shook his head in disbelief and then started to laugh, a great, huge, enormous, gigantic, tremendous, colossal, belly-shaking laugh that made him ripple from top to toe. Soon everyone else was laughing too.

"What are we laughing at?" Thomas said, still spluttering five minutes later.

"The wood is saved," Tamworth said.

The crowd cheered.

"But—but—the new route is to go right through the orchard and Pig House."

The crowd groaned.

"Why are you laughing then?" Thomas asked.

"I think it's funny that I did all that work to have it moved right through my house instead. I don't think I'll interfere next time."

"What are you going to do?"

"We shall do what we can to have it altered yet again, if only for the sake of Farmer Baggs's land. But, as for myself . . ."

He stretched his golden body till he seemed bigger than any pig that ever lived.

"Where Melanie is, where my friends are, that is my home, wherever it may be!"

Cheers rang out and he turned to go with his little pink and black pig and Blossom and Thomas.

"He doesn't half carry on," Hedgecock said to Mr. Rab. "All I can see is more work and trouble."

"And your trouble is that there's no poetry nor love in your soul. In fact, I doubt if you've got a soul. Don't hit me."

But Hedgecock hit Mr. Rab several times as they trotted along the way, following Tamworth Pig and the others.

Chapter Thirteen

———————————*———————————

"For goodness sake, Thomas, sit down."

"I can't."

"Well, stop wandering round the room. Read a book or play a game."

Daddy was being very patient for him, but Thomas continued to shuffle up and down, round and round.

"Look, boy, if you don't settle, you'll have to go to bed."

"I can't go to bed until I know."

"There's nothing to worry about. Piglets are being born all the time."

"But not Tamworth's piglets. They're special."

"Look at Blossom. She's just as excited as you are and she's sitting quietly reading."

Blossom stood up.

"I've read the same page twenty times and it still doesn't mean anything. Oh, Mummy, when shall we know?"

"It won't be long now. Come on, I'll make a drink and then you really will have to go to bed. It's almost midnight."

"I want to know how many," Thomas insisted.

"So do I," put in Hedgecock. "Fancy counting all those little trotters. Very interesting."

They all adjourned to the kitchen, including Daddy, and sat around the table.

"I can't wait," Thomas said.

"You say that every Christmas Eve. That's what tonight feels like, waiting for Christmas Day really to arrive. Or birthdays," Blossom replied.

Daddy stood up and yawned.

"Well, I'm off to bed and I think it would be a good idea if everyone else did, too."

He peered especially hard at Thomas.

"Please let us stay. Oh, Please. Please! PLEASE!"

"Farmer Baggs promised us he'd come," Thomas cried.

A loud knock rat-tatted at the door. The children rushed to open it and Farmer Baggs entered the kitchen, blinking in the bright light.

"I could see your lights were still on, so I thought I'd best let young Thomas and Blossom in on it."

"How many? How many? How many?" They danced round him.

Farmer Baggs's eyes were twinkling.

"Guess."

"Oh, no, don't tease us," Blossom cried.

"Eight," Thomas said.

Farmer Baggs shook his head.

"Ten," guessed Hedgecock.

"Fourteen," Thomas said, jumping up and down.

"No."

"Oh!" wailed Blossom. "There's only a few!"

"No, said Farmer Baggs.

"Eighteen," Thomas said, hopping on one leg.

"I give up. I can't bear it," Blossom whispered.

"I know! I know! I know!" Thomas shouted. "It's twenty, isn't it? Twenty piglets!"

Farmer Baggs nodded. "You're right, young Thomas."

"Twenty. Good heavens!" Mummy exclaimed.

Daddy went to a cupboard and brought out a bottle.

"Let's drink to the piglets, all twenty of them."

He filled up glasses for everyone. They raised them high.

"To Melanie, Tamworth and the twenty piglets," he toasted.

"To Melanie, Tamworth and the twenty piglets," they all replied.

Blossom's eyes shone like twin beacons.

"It's as good as Christmas."

"Better," Thomas shouted, turning a somersault on the floor.

"Mind now, I 'ope it stays at twenty."

Farmer Baggs's voice was serious.

"Why, what do you mean?" Mummy asked, full of quick concern.

"That last little un's very weak. It's the runt of the litter, all right, and it'll 'ave to be bottle-fed if it's to live. As a matter o' fact, we thought it was dead. Wasn't breathing at all. But Tamworth gave it the kiss o' life, and 'e kept on and on, 'e wouldn't give up 'ope, and in the end it gave a twitch and we wrapped un in a warm blanket and there it was, alive."

"Oh, poor little thing. Will it live?"

"I 'ope so, as otherwise, it's going to upset Tamworth summat terrible. 'E already thinks the world of that little black runt, he do."

"Black?" Daddy asked.

"Yes. As black as coal."

"What colour are the others?"

"We . . . ell, there's so many. But the first's a great, big, golden pig like Tamworth and there's lots more like 'im, and then there's some black and pink uns and some just pink uns, like all the colours o' the rainbow they are, but there's only one all black un, the runt."

"Oh, I want to see them, now," Blossom said.

"No, definitely not. Melanie and the piglets will need their sleep." Mummy's voice was firm.

"And so do Tamworth and I. Scoot, scatter, be off. You can see them in the morning."

Daddy's voice was even firmer so they went upstairs.

"I shall compose an extremely long poem about this," Mr. Rab decided.

"Ugh," Hedgecock growled.

"I shan't sleep," Thomas announced, settling Num around him in bed, and was thereupon struck by a terrible thought.

"You don't think I ought to give my Num to that little black piglet, do you? I don't really want to, but . . ."

"Shouldn't think it'd be much use to anyone but you really," Hedgecock, ever practical, said.

"Oh, good," yawned Thomas and fell asleep.

But Blossom lay awake thinking of the piglets and worrying about a small, black one who might not live till morning.

Despite their late night, the children arose early and without stopping for breakfast, though Blossom grabbed several chocolate biscuits as she went, they set out in the chilly Spring morning. Four months had passed since Melanie came, four months since they'd heard that the motorway was to cleave its way through Baggs's Farm and over Pig House, four months for Tamworth of unending speeches and meetings and delivering leaflets, but he was now a Pig filled with the strength of ten pigs because at the end of each day, Melanie was there to greet him with her gentle voice and loving ways. She did not come out and assist him, Thomas and Blossom did that as of old, but she was always ready at Pig House to greet the successful or comfort the downhearted.

But in the end it was all worthwhile. The Minister for the Environment visited Tamworth and it was decided that the motorway should take the original route after all, the one first chosen, through the slag heaps and the low-lying marshlands to the east. So at the end of March the digging, the clearing and the vast upheavals that accompany motorways began. The farm, Pig House and the damson tree and all the neighbourhood were safe.

By now, Melanie was enormous. She could hardly walk on her tiny trotters.

"It'll be funny if they're April Fool piglets," Thomas said.

"I don't fancy that," Tamworth sniffed, looking down his snout.

As a matter of fact they were born on 31st March,

but only just. The little black one arrived about an hour before midnight.

Tamworth was waiting for them, ears a-prick, bristles a-shine. He lifted his trotter to his mouth and shushed but it wasn't necessary. Blossom and Thomas were so much on tiptoe their feet hurt. They held two carrier bags, packed earlier, full of grapes and apples and cabbages. Nervous and excited, they entered the extra room built on to Pig House by Farmer Baggs for Melanie and the Piglets.

And there lay Melanie on her side, eyes closed, and curled against her was a warm, breathing, smooth sea of little bodies, almost too many to count. Thomas and Blossom and Hedgecock and Mr. Rab knelt down to touch the soft warmth. Melanie opened her eyes and looked proudly at her numerous offspring and smiled at them all.

"They're all real and complete. Look at their ears," Blossom breathed.

"It's their tails I like," Thomas said, touching a golden one.

The Welsh rabbit had crept in quietly beside them. "Primroses and celandines from the animals in the wood, brought you, I have," he murmured.

"Thank you," Melanie said.

"Shut up a minute," interrupted Hedgecock, that ungracious animal. "Flowers is no good to anyone. You've made me go wrong in my counting. I keep getting nineteen. Unless you've got one tucked under your tail, Melanie."

"Tamworth will show you the other one," she said.

The Pig of Pigs led them to the next room. There, on Tamworth's own bed, nestled in a soft blanket, surrounded by hot water bottles, lay the tiniest, funniest, ugliest, little pig ever.

"He's very small," Blossom said in surprise.

"Half the size of the others," Thomas added.

"A third I should say," Hedgecock surmised.

"Do you think he'll live?" squeaked Mr. Rab.

Hedgecock kicked him but Tamworth hadn't heard, for he was gazing with immense pride at his microscopic son.

"I saved him, you know. And he'll grow up to be a fine, big, noble pig, you'll see!"

There was a funny little noise rather like a snort of laughter from the sleeping animal, that made them all start in surprise.

"I wonder," thought Blossom. "I wonder."